Unhappily

This book is dedicated to the greatest man I have ever known, my dad,

Martin R. Silas

This book is a work of fiction. Any similarities of people, places, instances, and locals are coincidental and solely a work of the author's imagination.

Chapter 1

I laid as still as I could. I was pretending to be asleep to avoid having sex with my husband.

Again.

Don't get me wrong, Desmond's sex is okay.

It just isn't like the sex that I have with Tyrone.

"Baby, are you awake?" my husband begged in my ear.

Still, I just laid there. I threw in a light fake snore to convince him that I was in a deep sleep and that he shouldn't disturb me.

Softly, he released a sigh, just before kissing my head and rolling out of bed.

How did we get here?

I have no idea.

Desmond and I have been married for ten long years, and we dated for a few years before that. We have everything that everyone else wants. Great careers, three beautiful kids, a nice house, and luxury cars.

Desmond is as handsome as he's always been. He's just my type – brown-skinned, muscular, and everything else in between. I'm aging like fine wine, yet, still, for the past year or so, something has been missing, between us, at least that's what it felt like to me.

Desmond still walks around like he's the happiest man in the world, and as though I'm still the love of his life. Whereas I found myself in the arms and bed of another man that I know doesn't mean me any good.

I met Tyrone as I waited for my best friend, Dejah, at a bar one night. I was way out of his league, but he couldn't have cared less. He was bold. Cocky. And I understand why. Not only is he one of the sexiest men on God's green earth, but he also lays pipe like nobody's business. And he knows it too.

I still don't know why I gave him my number that night, but I did. And I've been stuck on him like a bee to a honeycomb ever since.

Sex with him is so addictive. Almost like a drug. I was always looking for my next fix. And now I've found it. I just can't seem to get enough of him.

And I knew that means that trouble is up ahead.

But I can't stop. It's as though I know fooling around with him is going to mess up my life, someday, but I don't care. Or maybe it's that I don't care enough.

Obviously, I want my family, my husband, my life. It's just…I'm fine with being a bad wife. For now, anyway.

Once I heard the water from the shower hit the bathtub floor, I found my thumping clitoris, and with Tyrone and his massive dick on my mind, I pleased myself.

Tyrone hasn't touched me in three days, and it felt like forever. My schedule at work has been crazy, and then Desmond has been a little clingier than usual, so getting away to sneak off to Tyrone hasn't been all that easy.

But I'm coming.

Oooh, and I'm cummin' too…

I came, hurried out of bed, and prepared to jump in the shower as soon as Desmond was done.

"Oh, good morning, baby," he said, entering our bedroom to find me looking in the closet.

"Good morning, handsome," I said.

Desmond approached me with his wet naked body.

After all these years, he's still in shape. His six-pack is the best thing about his body. His smooth honey-colored skin is a close second.

Desmond is very attractive, in his own unique way, especially now that he'd grown a full beard and kept a bald head. My brown-skin, short frame, and wide hips complemented him well. If I must say so myself, we do look damn good together.

We always have.

Suddenly, Desmond kissed me. I forced myself to kiss him back.

"I love you," he whispered.

"I love you more."

Desmond started to caress my outer thighs, but softly, I touched his hand.

"I have a meeting in less than an hour," I lied.

"All I need is three minutes," he smiled. "As bad as I want you, maybe just two."

I tried to think of another excuse, but there wasn't one. I was going to have to have sex with my husband. And I wasn't exactly happy about it.

Desmond didn't hesitate to bend me over inside our walk-in closet. I grabbed ahold of one of the metal bars and attempted to conceal my attitude. Impatiently, I waited for him to enter me.

Oooh...what's that?

Is that a new move?

Desmond's firm grip of my hips turned me on, but the swirls and the pounds that he was applying to my pussy from behind, nearly made me droll.

Has he been watching porn?

My eyes rolled into the back of my head.

Everything that he was doing felt good. Really good.

And I found myself biting my bottom lip and enjoying every bit of it.

I'm one hundred percent sure the usual routine sex between Desmond and I was part of the reason I started to fool around with Tyrone.

For quite some time now, sex with my husband had become somewhat of a second job that I only did because I had to. Or maybe it was more like a chore.

Our sex life lacked excitement most of the time, but at this moment, I was getting excitement, satisfaction, porno vibes, and a little bit of everything else in between.

I moaned loudly, which only motivated Desmond to pump harder. And for the first time, in a long time, together, we reached the finish line.

"Damn," I mumbled.

"What, baby?" Desmond huffed, slightly out of breath.

"That was good. I mean, it was really good."

"You want some more?" he smiled.

Shaking my head, I hurried to shower for my pretend meeting. If he keeps sexing me like this, maybe I'll stop sleeping with Tyrone.

For some reason, as the water hit my face, I thought about the first time Desmond and I made love.

We met our last year in college.

We didn't go to the same school, but we were both seniors. We were full of so many ideas and plans for the future. We developed a friendship before anything, and then on graduation night after we had spent time with our families, he told me that he was in love with me.

I told him that I loved him too.

And I did.

It was just something about him. I couldn't quite explain it. I remember us lying in his older brother's backyard on a blanket, looking up at the stars. Desmond looked at me and told me he was going to marry me one day. He told me that he was going to take care of me and give me everything I've ever wanted.

And then he kissed me.

I remember how I felt at that exact moment.

I felt warm. Safe. Full.

And then right there, without caring if we got caught, we made love for the first time, and I knew that I wanted to be with him forever.

And for a long time, I felt that way, I really did.

Even after marriage, and with kids, and careers, we somehow still found ways to give each other butterflies every now and then. We still found ways to please each other and make sure that we were putting in the work to have a successful marriage.

And then it came a day, where it all just stopped.

Sex started lasting for five minutes. There were only good morning, goodbye, and good night kisses. Most of our conversation had become about work, dinner, or the kids. And sometimes, he would barely notice if I did something different with my hair.

The excitement was just gone.

I know it's not an excuse to step out on him, and honestly, I never thought I would.

It just happened.

Tyrone just happened.

But the real problem is that he…we…*it*…keeps happening. And I don't want it to stop.

After getting myself dressed and the kids up and dressed, I kissed them all goodbye for the day.

It was Desmond's day to drop the kids at school, and because I'd lied about a meeting that I didn't have until later that day, I headed to get breakfast.

"Hey, girl, good morning. I thought your pregnant tail would still be asleep," I answered the phone for Nicole.

"I was, but Tierra woke me up."

Tierra was Nicole's best friend. Nicole was a friend I met through my best friend, Dejah. And now we all are pretty close and hang out all the time. We're friends, but more like sisters.

"Well, what's going on?"

"Nothing. I was calling you back from yesterday."

I exhaled. "Oh, yeah, I was calling to tell you something about your man…your baby daddy…your…David. I saw him with a woman on my lunch break yesterday. He didn't see me, but I snapped a picture of them together."

"Send it to me," Nicole huffed. And then, she started to curse. "I'm so sick of David's shit! Like if I could kill him and get away with it, I would! I swear to God I would!"

David and Nicole had only been fooling around for a few months before Nicole got pregnant. At first, he was nice and sweet. He was wining and dining her. Taking her on all of these expensive vacations. Nicole used to brag about him all the time, making us all wish we had a man like him. But as soon as she got that positive pregnancy test, everything changed. Or maybe it's just that he started to show his true colors.

"All he does is lie! That's it! Everything that comes out of his mouth is a goddamn lie! One minute, he wants us and he wants to be a family. The next minute, he doesn't want the baby, and he's out doing whatever he wants to do! I'm just so tired of him!"

Nicole started to cry. I knew it was the hormones because she was as tough as nails and wouldn't be crying otherwise.

"It's going to be okay, Nicole."

"I'm just ready for this pregnancy to be over. These four months can't go by fast enough. Honestly, I wished I'd gotten an abortion like I started to. Remember? I wasn't going to tell him about the pregnancy at all, because I wasn't sure I wanted to be somebody's mama. But no, I loved him. And he made it like he was so in love with me. I thought everything was going to be fine. If I had known things were going to turn out like this, I would've been at the clinic the same day I peed on the stick!"

I talked to her until she was done crying and offered to bring her breakfast. She declined. So, alone, I stopped to have breakfast at one of my favorite spots in Florida.

Big Mama's Backyard.

"What can I get you this morning, pretty lady?"

"Oh, she'll have eggs, scrambled, with a little cheese, buttered toast, three slices of turkey bacon, and a sweet tea, no ice," I heard behind me.

Tyrone.

Oooh! Tyrone!

"What are you doing here?" I looked around to make sure I didn't see anyone I recognized.

"The same reason you're here. Breakfast."

Tyrone sat down at the table.

Other than his good looks and good dick, Tyrone didn't have anything else going for himself. He was a six-foot, black as midnight, dread headed hustler. Smart-mouthed, cocky as hell, selling and slanging whatever he could. No real goals or dreams. An old truck and living with one of his friends.

He just isn't my type of man at all.

He's nothing like my husband.

Desmond is a successful architect. Very smart and ambitious. A man of his word. A man with goals and dreams that he's willing to work his ass off to achieve.

And speaking of...

"Des-Desmond," I stuttered as he approached the table.

My heart was beating so fast, that instinctively, I touched my chest.

"Hey, baby," Desmond looked at me, and then at Tyrone.

Tyrone looked at my husband completely unbothered.

"I came by to pick you up some breakfast since you said you had to rush to work for a meeting."

That's right. A meeting.

"Yes. Uh, yes. This is the meeting. We decided to have it over breakfast," I lied.

I was afraid to look at Tyrone.

Tyrone knew I was married, but he didn't care. And I wasn't sure if he would go along with my lie or not.

"Oh," Desmond mumbled.

"Yes. He has a really good story idea, so that's what we're talking about."

"That's not how it works, though, right? I mean, shouldn't the story be written already before having a meeting with you?" Desmond questioned.

I run a small publishing company.

It's always been my dream. Not to mention that I self-published three best-selling series that landed me on every store bookshelf, tons of publications, and on T.V.

Running my own small press was the next step in my journey, and for the past two years, everything has gone smoothly. None of my authors have had as much success as I have, but it's coming. I can feel it.

"Are you telling me how to do my job, Desmond?"

"I would never." My husband smiled just as the waiter brought over my drink. "Well, I guess you don't need breakfast then. Continue with your meeting. Call me when you can." Desmond leaned down to kiss me.

I kissed him in a hurry.

Still feeling as though I was going to faint, I watched my husband until he was out of sight.

"So..." Tyrone started. I almost forgot that he was still sitting there. "That's the husband, huh?" He smirked. "He has no idea about the shit that I do to his wife. Or the shit that I'm about to do to her."

I looked at Tyrone confused.

"I played along." Tyrone stood up. "Now, this meeting is over. I'm about to go fuck the shit out of you."

I don't know why, but immediately, I was turned on by his words. It was something about the way he talked to me. It was borderline disrespectful at times, but I liked it.

"And you know I like it when you wear your hair like that. Come on, so I can pull it."

I had my fluffy curls pulled back into a ponytail, showcasing my big brown eyes and fairly round face.

After dropping a few bucks on the table, without waiting for my breakfast, like a sprung high school girl, I followed Tyrone out of the restaurant with a smile on my face. And without a care in the world, I was on my way to cheat on my husband.

Again.

***

"Marriage isn't supposed to feel like this…right?" Dejah questioned.

I admired her chocolate skin as it seemed to shimmer in the sunlight. Dejah had a cute, teenage girl look about her. As though she wasn't older than sixteen.

"Girl, marriage is…" I huffed. "Marriage is tricky."

I finished typing a text to my husband, sent it, and then started texting Tyrone.

"I feel so trapped. I just want to live and have a little fun, you know. But now that we're all married and stuff, Tyree wants to change things up. All he wants to talk about is goals and the future. I mean, don't get me wrong, that's all good. But now that the boys are getting a little older, it gives me a little more freedom, you know. Hell, it gives us both more freedom. They were still pretty young when Tyree and I first got together. But the things I want to do, Tyree doesn't want to do them anymore."

"Well, I mean, it has been a long road to get y'all to this point. After all those years of being together, y'all just got married. Maybe what he wants is just what's best for all of you."

"What's best? Bitch, shut up. I know you're talking! You got a good ass husband at home, but it doesn't stop you from letting that ole' roughneck fuck your brains out, now does it?" Dejah laughed.

Of course, I'd told her about my affair with Tyrone. She's the only person I told. And she better not tell anyone else!

"Right. All I'm saying is that I don't know how we…I…got here. And I don't want you to get here either. It's not fun. I feel guilty all the time."

"But not guilty enough to stop."

"Unfortunately…no. I'm literally texting Tyrone right now to see when we can meet up again…"

Abruptly, we stopped talking as the other girls approached the table.

"Hey, y'all!" Tierra yelled.

Nicole groaned.

"Girl, damn, you still have a few months to go and you look like you're about to pop." Dejah rubbed her belly.

"I am. I just want it to be over."

I stared at her, wondering if she was going to bring up David.

She did.

"So, I confronted David," Nicole looked at me. "Of course, he got mad and tried to act like the chick he was with was just a friend."

"A friend, my ass."

"Right. So, now, I won't answer any of his calls or text messages. I just want him to leave me alone. For good. I want him completely out of my life. So much so that I'm thinking about…" Nicole paused. "I'm thinking about putting the baby up for adoption."

"What!" Tierra yelled.

"I'm just tired of him. He doesn't really even want the baby. He just uses that I'm pregnant by him when he wants some ass. I'm just so stressed out."

"We got you. We all got you. I'll take the baby if you still feel this way once she's born."

I rolled my eyes at Dejah. "Weren't you just screaming about enjoying your freedom? What are you going to do with another baby? Furthermore, what is your husband going to say about this?" I smirked. Dejah rolled her eyes.

"But as she said, we got you, Nicole. Screw David. You got us. All of us."

"Thanks, y'all."

We enjoyed our weekly lunch for the next two hours.

We've been getting together at least once a week for over a year now, and it was something that we all looked forward to. There's nothing like meeting up to just vent with your girlfriends about what's going on.

"Take your ass home, Bailey!"

"Okay, okay, okay! I am."

I hit the alarm on my candy apple red Lexus, and once inside, I texted Tyrone and told him I was going home to my husband.

The whole drive home, I was tempted to turn around.

Tyrone is like a drug.

I crave him. I want him all the time, and I don't know how to make it all go away.

"Hey, pretty lady, how was your day?" Desmond greeted me with a kiss. "I'm making dinner tonight. You can relax, go read or write, or do whatever you want to do for the rest of the day. I got the kids. You just go and do you." Desmond walked away.

Other women would kill for a husband like Desmond.

What in the hell is wrong with me?

He cooks and cleans. He's a great father. He believes in sharing the load. I don't deserve him.

Whatever we were going through could be fixed. The little things that he does daily remind me that stepping out on him just isn't worth losing him.

My affair with Tyrone was a stupid, stupid mistake.

As much effort as I'm putting into having an affair, I could be putting into getting our marriage back on track.

And I was going to start.

Right here. And right now.

"Desmond?" I screamed after him.

"Yes?" He turned around.

"Um, there is something that I want to do…. but I need your mouth to do it."

Desmond smiled as big as the morning sun. I could tell that he was shocked. It's been such a long time since I've come on to him.

"Well, I'm at your service," he said, knowing exactly what I was referring to.

Genuinely, I smiled at him.

I love my husband.

I love my husband.

I love…my…husband…but…

I love how Tyrone makes me feel too.

After an hour of making love, which turned out to be just as good as the last time, surprisingly, I vowed that I was going to cut Tyrone off for good.

I texted him and told him I didn't want to see him anymore. He responded by calling me a liar and sent me a picture of his thick, black dick.

And then he told me to come to see him---now.

I said no. And I meant it. Still, after a few more text messages back and forth with Tyrone, I found myself lying to Desmond about running to the store and headed Tyrone's way twenty minutes later.

I was just going to talk to him. That's it.

"I'm serious about what I said," I said to Tyrone as soon as he opened his front door.

His house was full of people.

Tyrone stepped outside, closing the door behind him.

"Oh, yeah? You're serious?" Tyrone came closer to me.

"Ye…ye…yes. I am."

Tyrone chuckled as he kissed my lips.

Instinctively, I kissed him back.

"Then, why are you here?"

"I came to tell you that I was done."

"You not done until I say you done," Tyrone smiled at me. "I can't wait to taste you. Can I taste you?"

Tyrone kissed my lips again.

"Bailey?"

I heard my name behind me.

It was my friend Tierra.

"Tyrone?"

I looked at him and then back at her.

"Uh, I'll leave y'all to it," Tierra turned around and walked away. I chased after her.

"Wait, Tierra! Wait!"

"You're cheating on Desmond? With Tyrone?"

"You know Tyrone?" I asked her without answering her question.

"Yes. We've gone on a date or two. He told me he was single. Well, I guess he is since the woman he is obviously screwing is married."

Tierra sounded disgusted.

Tierra Smith, or Tee Tee as the kids call her, is a little older than the rest of us. She's a 35-year-old, amazing hairstylist and single mom who is still looking for Mr. Right. Since I've known her, she's found several Mr. Wrong's, but she hasn't given up on love yet.

I'm surprised she would even date someone like Tyrone, but then again, he is a charmer and has a way of getting you to do whatever he wants you to do.

"I texted Tyrone earlier and told him I might stop by. He told me to come through anytime. Bailey, why are you doing this to Desmond? He's such a good guy."

"I know, Tierra. I know."

"And with Tyrone? I mean, I'm single and maybe even a little desperate, but you. You have no business dealing with someone like Tyrone."

"I know. I was actually coming here to tell Tyrone that whatever we had going on is over. That kiss should've never happened. He kissed me."

"Seems like you didn't want him to stop," Tierra pointed out. "Look, you're my girl, and that's your business. I just don't want you to end up losing everything you have behind…nothing. But it's your life. I love you. I definitely won't be seeing Tyrone anymore, after seeing… Um, just call me," she said. Tierra hugged me, but I could feel the judgment seeping out of her skin.

I stood on the sidewalk until Tierra drove away. I noticed that Tyrone didn't come after either of us.

Tierra is right.

I should've never been here in the first place.

So, I got into my car and drove away, vowing to never cheat on my husband again.

At least I'm going to try.

***

Chapter 2

"He's what?"

"Married," Nicole repeated. "He's been married for eight long years! He's been married this whole time! His wife's name is Staci, and they have two kids!"

All of us sat with our mouths hanging wide open.

"And check this out, the woman in the photo that you sent me…that's not his wife either! I guess she's just some other chick that he's fooling around with. She probably doesn't know the truth about him either."

Nicole looked as though she was going to be sick.

"I'm having a baby by a married man," she whined.

"But you didn't know. It isn't your fault."

"It doesn't change the facts, Dejah. It doesn't change the facts," Nicole started to cry. "What am I going to do? This is so embarrassing! I feel so disgusted! I'm a lot of things, but I'm not a homewrecker. I would've never ever slept with him had I known he had a wife! And had she never called my phone, I would've never known."

"How did she get your number?"

"She said she went through the phone numbers of his phone bill. She said I was one of three women that he's currently cheating on her with. And when I told her I was pregnant, she started to cry. And then she said she would never accept my baby. Straight like that. She didn't sugarcoat it. She said David made plenty of money to pay me child's support, but that she wasn't leaving him and that she would never accept my child or allow my child around her children."

"I like her," Dejah mumbled. Tierra elbowed her.

"It's not my fault. I didn't know. I want this baby out of me!" Nicole's sudden yell startled me. "Now! Get it out! Get it out!"

Nicole started to push down on her stomach. Everyone else talked at her, but I grabbed her and held her close.

"I hate him! I hate him!"

"I know. I know you do. But that precious little girl in your belly is a blessing. She's innocent. And she was meant to be here, otherwise, you wouldn't be pregnant right now. Screw David, okay. Screw him. She's the only thing you need to be concerned about." I touched her belly. "You got this, Nicole. You are stronger than this. You will get through this."

Nicole didn't believe me. She sobbed louder and louder and turned as red as an apple. Nicole was high-yellow, as the old folks called it. A redbone, with long hair and a killer body. She was average looking, but of course, her assets, or should I say her ass, got her tons of attention from men. Surprisingly, usually, Nicole liked to be single. She liked having options. And then she met David. And though they were just kicking it, she started talking about settling down. I think she thought he was the one in the beginning. He was the one alright. The one who came into her life and turned it upside down. The one she should've stayed away from. The one that has changed her life forever.

The other women finally came in close to hug Nicole.

As we hugged her, I could feel Tierra staring at me. We haven't spoken much since she saw me at Tyrone's that night.

The look on her face was as though she was telling me that I could be Nicole. Or that there were so many women facing Nicole's situation, yet my ungrateful ass was cheating on a good man.

I get it.

I get it.

I get it!

I really do.

Since that night, I've been trying to get myself together. I only met up to have sex with Tyrone twice, and each time, I initially went to meet him to tell him that I was done. The first time, as I was talking, he pulled my pants down and started eating my pussy mid-sentence. The second time, I barely said two words before he was all over me. The funny thing is, before, I felt like I needed to be pleased by Tyrone. But here lately, since sex with Desmond was better times ten, the cravings for Tyrone were slowly but surely going away.

After we calmed Nicole down, Tierra offered to take her home with her. She said they would be back to get her car that next morning. Once they drove away, Dejah and I sat down on my front porch.

It was late summer. The weather was nice this time of year in Florida. It was the perfect day to take a drive to the beach to lay out on the sand in the sun.

"Man, I'm going to go home and fuck the shit out of Tyree tonight," Dejah commented out of nowhere.

I couldn't help but laugh.

"I'm serious, though. Man, I don't know what I would've done if I was in Nicole's shoes. Pregnant, by a man who has lied about being married the whole time. The shit is a disgrace. Not to mention…embarrassing! It really makes you appreciate what you have at home, you know?"

"Yeah. I know," I mumbled.

"So…no more Tyrone?" Dejah looked at me with the side-eye.

"No. No more Tyrone."

"Are you sure?"

"Yes, I'm sure. I feel bad. I've been trying to cut him off for the past few days, but after today, I'm done. I can't imagine Desmond cheating on me. I can't imagine finding out Desmond had a child on the way by another woman. That would break me. So, if I don't want it done to me, I damn sure shouldn't be doing it to him."

"That's right. That's my girl."

We talked for a while longer about our marriages and our kids. And once Dejah left, I called Desmond to see where he was. It was a Thursday, and usually, he was home from work by now.

Desmond didn't answer his phone, and with the kids staying over at my parent's house for the night, I headed inside to take a long, hot bath.

On top of the crazy personal life stuff that had been happening over the past few weeks, work was also a little hectic.

Running a publishing company is no easy task, and I was starting to think that I might need to hire a little more help to lighten the load.

I recently signed four new authors, all with amazing projects that would need tons of time and attention to make it perfect. And on top of everything else, I was ready to write a new book. I had the perfect idea for a new series, and I was eager to get back to writing. I just had to find the time.

"Desmond, is that you?" I screamed from the bathroom.

"Yes, it's me."

I smiled.

"How was your day? You're home late."

"My day was…interesting."

At the sound of his words and the tone of his voice, I sat up in the bathtub.

"What's wrong?"

Desmond appeared in front of the bathroom door.

"Are you cheating on me?"

My heart dropped.

"Wh---what?"

Desmond walked inside the bathroom and leaned up against the sink.

"I got this strange phone call today."

I tried to steady my breathing. I didn't want to look guilty.

"It was a woman. A voice I don't recognize. She said your wife is a whore. And then she hung up."

"What?"

Who the fuck would call Desmond and say something like that?

"At first, I didn't think anything of it. But as the day went on, I started to think about it. For a while there, you were acting a little strange. Most times, you barely want me to touch you. Some days, you don't even seem to be present. So…"

"Desmond, I'm not cheating on you. It was a cruel prank or something, but I'm all yours, baby. I promise."

"Okay," he smiled.

He believed me. Just like that. No more questions asked.

"Is that why you were late?"

"Oh no, a meeting ran over at work, and then I left my charger at home this morning, so my phone died just as we were finishing up."

I smiled at him. "The kids are gone. So, when I get out of this bathtub…"

Desmond leaped with excitement as he headed out of the bathroom.

I exhaled quietly.

Who would call Desmond's job, and call me a whore?

Tierra crossed my mind.

No. She wouldn't do that. She's my friend. And though she didn't like what I was doing, she wouldn't do something so foul.

Right?

Not to mention, Desmond said he didn't recognize the voice.

But who else would know where Desmond work to get in contact with him to say something like that?

Dejah most definitely wouldn't do that. We're best friends.

Thoughts flooded my mind as I washed my body.

Finally, stepping out of the bathtub, I concluded that whoever called my husband had better stay the hell out of my business, my marriage, and out of my way!

***

"He asked me about it, Tyrone!"

Tyrone smiled.

He told me that he'd gotten his friend's girlfriend to call Desmond's job and call me a whore. He said that he was just trying to get my attention since I hadn't returned his calls or text messages in a few days. He said he could feel me slipping away.

"That was childish!"

"So, I missed you. And you wouldn't answer any of my calls," Tyrone shrugged.

I hated that I'd told him anything about my husband. I couldn't even remember why I'd told him where Desmond worked in the first place. I shouldn't have told him I was married at all, but I think at the time, I thought it would make him second guess fucking me.

It didn't.

"I miss you."

"After that stunt, you pulled, I don't have anything else to say to you! If I wanted my husband to know about my affair, I would've told him myself! But as I've been trying to tell you for days, I'm done with this. I don't want to do this anymore. I want my marriage. I want my husband. I want my kids. It was fun while it lasted, but I'm done. Tyrone, I won't contact you again."

I tried to walk away, but he grabbed my arm.

"Bailey, this ain't just about you," he said. "I give you want you need. You give me what I want. And I want you. What makes you think you can drop me whenever the fuck you feel like it? I can have you whenever I want you. You told me that, remember? And I still want you. So, I'm going to have you."

"No, you can't! I'm done!"

Tyrone chuckled. "We're done when I say we're done. So, what I gotta' do, huh? Break up your little happy home to get you back in my bed?"

I tried to read his facial expression.

"What? You want me to send him some of these pictures of your pussy and titties that I got on my phone? Is that what I gotta' do to get you to fuck me?"

He sounded crazy!

"Just leave me alone. That's all I want."

"You don't want that."

"Yes, I do."

Tyrone walked closer to me. "No, you don't. You're just upset. I said sorry. Just don't ignore me like you did, and everything will be fine." He was so close that I could almost taste the gum that he was chewing. "I'll give you a few days to get over being upset. And then, I expect a call from you, Bailey."

Tyrone winked at me, and without looking back at me, he walked away.

I rushed inside my building and into my office.

What in the world have I gotten myself into?

Desmond hadn't asked me about the phone call again. It was as though he didn't believe that I would be capable of cheating on him. I guess that's a good thing. But for the past few days, I felt like I had to step up my "wife-game."

I was fucking him every chance I got and doing everything I could to make sure that he didn't have any doubts in his mind. It was as though the phone call to him was my wake-up call. It made me realize that no matter how bored I may have become, I still want to be with my husband. I still want my marriage.

So, Tyrone and I are over.
And I mean it this time!

I tried to force the thoughts of my husband and Tyrone out of my mind, but I couldn't seem to shake the feeling that something was going to go terribly wrong.

Unless…

Picking up my phone, I pressed the phone icon beside Tierra's name.

She allowed the phone to ring a few times before answering.

"Hey, girl," she said, once she answered. She sounded a lot happier than I expected her to.

"Hey, I was just calling because I know things have been weird between us lately. I was just thinking about it, and it's time we just completely forgot about that night."

"Oh, I have. We're all good. I just want what's best for you. And I don't want you to make a terrible mistake. That's all."

"I know you do. But I meant what I said. I don't talk to Tyrone anymore, so feel free to continue doing whatever it is that you guys were doing."

I figured if I could keep Tyrone busy with Tierra, then maybe he would leave me alone. Sure, it was somewhat nasty, I guess since I'd already been with him, and Tierra and I are friends, but it was a possibility that they've already fooled around in the first place. I never even bothered to ask.

"No. I'm good. Honey, I don't want your leftovers. Not leftovers like Tyrone, anyway. Now, Desmond Leftovers…that's a different story!" Tierra laughed.

"Okay, now, watch yourself!"

"Nah, seriously. Tyrone isn't the type of man I want or need. He approached me, and I thought, shoot, why not? But I'm talking to this new guy, so I guess we'll see how this goes."

Tierra was always looking for love.

She wanted it so badly. More than anything in the world. To the point where sometimes, it made her blind to the obvious. And once, it almost put her child in danger.

She was previously dating this guy, who had everything on her list. She truly thought he was the one. He was nice, successful, and she said the sex was good.

But there was a catch…not only was he attracted to her. But apparently, he had an eye for her daughter too. He'd tried to molest Tierra's daughter one night when she wasn't home, and it took her a long time to forgive herself.

She did. Eventually. And for a while, she swore off men, but that didn't last long.

She wants to be loved.

And for her sake, I sure hope she finds the love that she wants so much one day.

Tierra is super attractive. She's the prettiest of all of us. Brown-skinned, tall and skinny, with beautiful eyes and teeth. So, getting a man to notice her was never the problem. It was getting a man to love her the way she wanted to be loved that seemed to be a hassle. And though I love her, she was part of her own problem.

Tierra drove men away sometimes. She was always in love too fast. Too clingy. She almost came off like a mother-figure to them. Always telling them what to do, and wanting to know their every move, every second of the day. Once, I tried to tell her that maybe she was part of the problem. Maybe she was the reason that she couldn't keep a man, but that conversation didn't go so well. She didn't think that she had problems. So, I just let her continue to do her own thing. That's all I could do.

"Hopefully, this new guy will be "the" guy," I encouraged her. "You deserve everything you've ever wanted in a man. I really hope things work out."

"Hopefully. And maybe you and Desmond should try counseling. My clients talk about it all the time. I hear it helps."

We spoke a little while longer until her next appointment arrived, and then she was gone.

I'd thought about counseling a while ago, but I didn't feel that Desmond would want to go. Most folks that we know don't believe in getting a therapist. They don't see the point in letting a stranger in your business. They simply say go to church and give your problems to God. Desmond thinks this way as well. But I was going to definitely go to a few counseling sessions. Maybe it would help, and it certainly doesn't hurt to ask.

I'm not sure if I'll ever admit to the affair, but it would provide a safe space to tell him about the other things that were bothering me about our marriage lately. And maybe he had some things that he wanted to bring up and discuss too. Either way, I was definitely going to look into it.

I managed to move my personal issues to the side to focus on work for the rest of the day. I read an entire manuscript submission, and I absolutely loved it. Not to mention, it gave me a few ideas on how to spice up my marriage.

Later that evening, leaving only the cleaning crew in the building, I headed to my car. It was to no surprise that Tyrone was standing beside it.

"Go away."

"No," he smiled. "I was going to give you a few days to cool off, but then I thought about it. I want you. And I want you now."

"Tyrone, I told you, what we had is over."

"And I told you…no," he came closer to me. "I want you. And I'm going to have you. Right now…"

I rolled my eyes at him.

Tyrone unlocked the doors of his 2006 white Suburban.

"Get in the car."

"No. I told you, I want to try and save my marriage."

"You can do that…and me," Tyrone grinned.

"No, I can't!"

Tyrone huffed. "Okay, okay, okay. Just one last time for the road. And I'll leave you alone."

I shook my head no, but my body appeared to be down for one last ride.

"Come on, you know you want to."

I glanced around the empty parking lot. The cleaning crew's van was the only other vehicle there, and they would be inside for at least another hour or two.

"If I do this…this is it. No more. I mean it. Okay?"

"Fo'sho," Tyrone grinned, greedily.

Seconds later, I found myself mounting Tyrone's dick in the backseat of the truck, but for the first time, I felt guilty. I actually felt bad about having sex with him. And I knew right then that this was indeed the last time.

"Damn, you always get me right," Tyrone slapped my ass as I scrambled to find my panties. "Same time tomorrow? Shit, it can be the same place if you want it to be."

"What? Hell no. I meant what I said. I'm done."

I didn't give him a chance to respond. I got out of the truck, pulled down my skirt, and rushed to my car. Hurriedly, I fixed my hair before pulling off and headed to the grocery store.

I planned on cooking Desmond's favorite for dinner. Meatloaf, mac, and cheese, with spicy cabbage on the size.

Self-conscious because I was almost certain that I smelled like sex, I got out of my car and practically ran inside the grocery store.

"Umph," I groaned as soon as I noticed him.

David.

The father of my friend Nicole's baby.

"Are you his wife…Staci?" I boldly asked the woman on his arm.

"His wife? Staci? No. I'm Michelle." She pulled away from David.

"Oh, well, he has a wife, kids, a girlfriend, and a baby girl on the way."

David looked as though he wanted to choke me, but that didn't last long.

Michelle slapped the look right off his face.

"You lying, cheating bastard! Don't you ever call me again!" She turned her attention to me. "Thank you."

"It was my pleasure."

I rolled my eyes at David and walked away. The smile quickly faded once I realized that it could've been me.

Only in reverse.

God, I'm never cheating again.

Never.

I made it home to cook for my family.

"Baby, this lasagna is so good."

"Thank you. I made it with love."

The kids cleaned their plates and asked to be excused.

"I love you."

"I love you, too," Desmond said.

And then he started to talk about work.

I tuned him out and started to think about my first book serious.

I wrote "Rhythm and Romance" just three months after Desmond and I got married. I was so full of love, so inspired. The book was full of love and moments and memories that I shared with him. I poured my soul into writing it. I filled it with my happiness. I remembered how I felt back then. The mind frame I was in. How full of life, love, and hope I was. I thought I could do anything. I thought I could be anything. No dream was too big or small, and it was all because I had Desmond by my side.

I remember the day I got married, and the words my grandmother spoke to me. She saw exactly what I saw in Desmond.

"That man is going to love you and take care of you. He's going to give you everything that he has to give, and together, the two of you will be unstoppable." My grandmother said to me. "Do your part. Always show up for him like I'm sure he will show up for you. And your life will be just fine."

"Bailey? Are you listening?"

"Yes, babe. I'm listening," I lied.

My mother was right. Desmond turned out to be everything I'd hoped he would be.

"So, babe, I think we need to get away soon. Just me and you. What do you think?"

"Sounds good to me. It's been a while."

"It sure has. So, okay, finish telling me about your project…"

***

Chapter 3

"No, no, no!"

I double-checked the date.

My period is seven days late.

My period is never late.

"Maybe it's just stress. Yeah, it makes sense."

The past few weeks have definitely been full of stress. Everything was going crazy at work with deadlines. Desmond and I had started going to counseling, and he wasn't exactly happy about it. He was offended that I had so many problems with our marriage. I found out that after all these years, he was still genuinely happy with me, and I felt like an idiot to have but my marriage on the line. He literally sat in counseling and told the therapist that he loved everything about me. He didn't have any problems with me and our marriage and that he was fine with the way things are. He said whatever I wanted to do, he would do, and whatever made me happy, made him happy too. And it was obvious that he was serious, which made me feel even worse.

And David had shown up at Nicole's house, causing a scene behind the stunt that I'd pulled in the grocery store about two weeks ago. They ended up getting into a heated argument that ended with him going to jail and Nicole putting too much stress on the baby. Now she's on bed rest.

And shall I even mention Tyrone?

He just won't leave me alone.

At this point, he's basically forcing me to have sex with him to keep him from telling Desmond about our affair.

Needless to say, sex with him no longer gives me chills. These days, it makes me sick on my stomach. And I was currently weighing my options on whether or not I should just tell Desmond the truth.

"It's just stress. It's just stress."

"What's just stress?" Desmond entered the bathroom. My first instinct was to lie, but I didn't.

"My period is late. I'm sure it's just stress."

"Stress from me?" Desmond questioned. He questioned himself a lot lately.

"No, Desmond. Stop that. I told you, you're perfect. I just felt like we were just in a routine the past few years. That's all."

"All you had to do was say that. You didn't have to make a brotha' go to counseling just to tell him that you want to spice things up around here."

"Counseling is a good thing. It's helping us. I actually really like going. And I appreciate you going with me."

I flushed the toilet and then kissed his lips.

"Anything to make you happy," Desmond groaned.

"Oooh, I love it when you talk dirty to me," I joked.

My phone started to ring, just as Desmond opened his mouth to say something nasty.

I found my ringing phone on the bed, and immediately, I rolled my eyes.

Tyrone.

I'd blocked his number, but all he did was call me from other numbers. And I knew he was just going to keep calling me over and over again if I didn't answer.

He was most definitely one of the biggest mistakes of my life. If not the biggest.

"Hello," I tried to sound professional.

"Where you at?"

"Sorry, I'm out of the office today," I said just as Desmond entered the room.

"Oh, ole' boy must be close by. Well, ask him if I can borrow his wife in about an hour."

"Uh, I'll have to check my schedule."

"See you in an hour," Tyrone said before hanging up.

I hate him.

I really, really, hate him.

"What's wrong, baby? I can see it on your face."

"I'm so behind. I have deadline after deadline, and…"

Desmond kissed me while I was talking. "Relax. You got this. You're going to get it all done. Everything is going to be okay."

I exhaled.

"Okay."

"I love you."

"I love you, too."

"Go ahead to the office. We can hang out another day."

"No. We both took a day off to spend time together, and that's just what we are going to do."

I wasn't sure if Tyrone would really tell Desmond about our affair. After all, he did have someone call Desmond's job once, but I was going to have to take this chance.

Desmond is my first priority.

He has to be.

So, for the next few hours, Desmond and I enjoyed the day together. We drove to the next city over. We had lunch, went shopping, and even managed to have sex in the bathroom at the mall.

It was all Desmond's idea and just what the doctor ordered. The type of spontaneity that I was missing and longing for. It was just the type of effort I needed to remember why my marriage and Desmond was so important.

Tyrone only called twice, but he'd sent tons of text messages. Most of them threats. He talked to me as though I should be scared of him. And as though he owned me.

And though his text messages were rude and disturbing, they helped me to make up my mind. I'm going to have to tell Desmond about the affair. And I'm going to tell him at our next therapy session. I was going to beat Tyrone at his own game, and just tell my husband the truth.

I knew it was the only way to get Tyrone out of my life for good.

"I really had a good day today," I smiled at Desmond.

"Me too. I'm kind of glad we decided to go to therapy."

"Really?"

"Yeah. I wouldn't have known you needed extra time and attention otherwise. I'm glad you wanted to work through things versus going out here and sleeping around on me. The thought of another man touching you makes me want to kill somebody! That shit would've been unforgivable."

I swallowed the lump in my throat.

Unforgivable?

Did he just say unforgivable?

"Whoa, kill somebody, huh? And unforgivable."

"Hell yeah. You're mine. I couldn't imagine another man putting his hands on you."

Desmond took a sip of his drink, and so did I.

Hmm...Maybe I shouldn't tell him after all.

But I can't fool around with Tyrone forever.

Telling Desmond is the only way.

Right?

With the word unforgivable playing over and over again in my head, as Desmond continued to talk as I pulled out my cellphone and did what I felt I had to do.

At least for now.

And feeling defeated, I responded to Tyrone's messages.

***

"Of course, you can stay here," I moved out of the way to let Dejah and her kids inside. "Go check out our new game room," I smiled at Dejah's pre-teen boys, Jerod and

James. Once they were out of sight, I turned my attention to Dejah.

"What happened?"

Dejah shook her head. "He's smothering me! I just can't take it anymore!"

"What does that mean?"

"I don't know. I don't know," Dejah repeated. "Tyree just wants so much more from me these days. It's like I can't breathe when I'm around him anymore. And on top of everything, he lost his job yesterday. He loved that damn job. And no, that's not why I left him. He'll find another job. I'm sure. He just kept going on and on and finding every little fault in me, because he was let go. And trying to tell me what I need to do, and that I needed to be doing more. I just had to get out of there."

Dejah was what I called a free-spirit. She was always bouncing from here to there. From job to job. She had two degrees and didn't use either of them. She would work a job for a few months or a year, get bored, and quit to try something else. Most say it's a Sagittarius thing, but I can see how it could be a little frustrating to a spouse who wants to plan for the future.

I sat next to my friend.

"I know I'm a bit much sometimes. I know I'm indecisive and that I like change. But I'm trying. I've been trying to be calmer and more stable, but that's just not who I am. Tyree knew that before he married me. And I'm not changing who I am. Not for him. Not for anyone."

"I'm sure he just wants the best for all of you."

"I get that. I do. He just needs to back the fuck off a little."

"Well, you guys can stay here as long as you need to. There's plenty of room."

I knew Desmond wouldn't mind.

Speaking of...

"Hey, Dejah, nice to see you," he said as he kissed my forehead.

I followed him towards our bedroom.

"Hey, Dejah needs to stay here for a little while. Is that okay?"

"Sure. Is everything going to be alright?"

"I hope so."

Desmond walked by me, and a whiff of a fruity perfume tickled my nose.

"Hmm, that assistant of yours must've been around a lot today."

Desmond turned around. "Nope. She was off today. Why?"

"Oh, I figured she was around because you smell like perfume."

I watched his facial expression and his body language. Although I was having an affair on him, still, it never crossed my mind how I would feel if Desmond was stepping out on me.

"Hmm, I didn't notice. Maybe it's from working with Taylor. We're working on something big together."

Desmond headed into the bathroom, and the next sound I heard was the water hitting the bathtub floor.

I had no reason to think that he was lying.

But what if he is?

Nah, not Desmond.

He loves me too much.

I was the one out here being a whore.

Out of nowhere, I started to think about my parents.

My parents have been married for thirty-five years. And as far as I know of, both of them have had at least one affair on each other. My mother stepped out on my father first. I remember overhearing one of their conversations. I had to be around twelve years old, and I remember hearing my mother confess to my dad the love she had for the other man. I'll never forget the words my father said to her.

He told my mother: "We both know that it takes a hell of a lot more than love to make a marriage work. We love each other, maybe a little less than we did back in the day, but it's still love. Yet, it takes a whole lot more than just love to make this marriage work. What we have here is good. But if you want to throw it away, I won't stop you."

After their conversation that night, I caught my mother crying every day, for three days after that. And on the fourth day, she cooked this big feast, and when my father walked in from worked that night, she kissed him like never before. I knew right then that she was choosing him. She was choosing her family.

My father, on the other hand, he didn't step out on my mother until we were all grown and out of the house. My mother called it a mid-life crisis. And after months of doing whatever it was that he wanted to do, he was back home with my mother as though nothing had ever happened.

I remember telling myself as I walked down the aisle towards Desmond that I would never be my mother and father. I told myself that I would never get tired of my marriage or get tired of loving the man of my dreams.

Yet, I ended up being more like my parents than I wanted to be.

"Bailey? Girl, what are you thinking about?" Dejah snapped her fingers in my face.

"Life," I half-smiled. "Crazy, complicated life."

"Hmph. Tell me about it."

***

"My period hasn't come on."

"What does that have to do with me?" Tyrone questioned.

"Nothing at all. Trust me. I would do what needs to be done if…"

I was terrified of taking a pregnancy test, but I knew that I had to. I was now weeks past due for my cycle, and there wasn't a cramp in sight.

"Good. Cause' I don't want any kids," Tyrone smiled.

The same smile that used to make my panties moist, now made me want to gag.

"You know what..." I pulled my curly hair into a ponytail. "I'm telling my husband about our affair at counseling tonight. This...whatever this was at one point, is dead. This is over. I'm coming clean, and I would appreciate it if you never call me again."

Tyrone laughed behind me. "Stop trippin' baby. You know how I feel about you. I'll call you later."

I slammed the door.

I'm telling Desmond.

Today.

It was lunchtime, and before heading back to work, I decided to stop to get a salad.

"Nicole?"

She stopped kissing David and looked at me as though she was a deer caught in headlights.

"Hey, Bailey."

"Why are you here with him? You do remember his wife, right?"

Nicole looked embarrassed.

"It's...complicated."

"No, it isn't. He's married. A liar. And a cheater. That isn't complicated, Nicole. He has taken you through pure hell. Hell, you can't even go to work now because of him."

I had my own mess going on, but David made my skin crawl. He just doesn't deserve a woman like Nicole.

"Look, back off. She's grown," David butted in. "She's the mother of my child. If we want to kick it, that's our business. She's a grown ass woman. Now, she knows the truth, and she knows what she's getting herself into."

Nicole looked back at David.

"Well, baby, you know what I mean."

Nicole touched her belly and then looked at me ashamed.

"Can you take me home?"

"I sure can."

"Nicole, really? You're going to let her whack ass come in here and make you leave like you're some little ass girl or something?" David yelled.

Without looking back, Nicole mumbled the words, "Goodbye, David."

I helped her inside my car, and for a while, we rode in silence.

"I know, I'm stupid," Nicole finally said.

"You're not stupid."

"Yes, I am. And the strange thing is I hate him, yet somehow love him all at the same time," she sounded disappointed. "But he lied about being married. And it's clear that he isn't leaving her. Yet, my mind, in some way, hopes that he does. It's like, for months, I kept telling myself that once I had the baby, he was going to do this big transformation and go back to the man that he was when I first met him. But that person was a lie. Everything about him is a lie. He's with the woman he wants to be with. He married her. I'm just his something extra. That's all I've ever been."

"You're too good for him anyway."

Nicole didn't respond.

"You are. You have so much to offer, and he knows that. That's why he's trying to keep you in this situation, but you're better than this."

I was talking to her, but I was listening to my own advice. No one is going to force me to keep doing something that I don't want to do.

"You are going to be okay. You have to believe that."

"Okay," was all Nicole said.

I got her home and helped her to get scttled before finally heading back towards my office.

"Your two o'clock is already here."

"Okay, send him in."

A few moments later, in walked Michael C. Scales.

"I've been watching you," I smiled at him.

He looked even better in person.

Tall, brown-skinned, low fade, and a full bcard.

"Thank you for giving me this opportunity."

"I like your style. Your self-published books have a lot of reviews and create a lot of buzz. It's time to take you to the next level."

"I can get with that," he said, taking a seat in front of me. "I did my research on you too."

"Good. I like a man who knows who he's getting into bed with…well, so to speak."

He smiled. "I've had a few big companies try to pick me up. I wasn't a fan of their terms. And I figured since I was making enough noise and money without them, I didn't need them. But you…it's something about you and your company." Michael said.

"Well, let's talk business, shall we?"

"So, sorry! A meeting ran over, but I'm here!" I yelled hours later as I took my seat on the couch next to Desmond.

"Nice of you to join us," our therapist, Joanne, smiled.

I smiled at Desmond. He frowned.

"Um, before we get started, there's something that I want to say," I turned to face Desmond.

I was about to come clean about Tyrone. I was scared, but I knew it had to be done. Considering that Tyrone was yet again, blowing up my phone as though he owned me or something.

Enough is enough.

"Um, so at one point in time, as you know, I was feeling…"

"You had an affair," Desmond interrupted me. He shook his head. "Yeah, I ran into ole' buddy today. Well, actually, he ran into me. You know, the one I saw you having breakfast with that time. Imagine my surprise when he told me that the two of you have been fucking around for a while. He said he didn't know about me until that day."

"Wait! No! That's not true! He knew from the very beginning that I was married!"

"Oh, so it is true? You were cheating on me? Huh?" Desmond screamed suddenly. "You were cheating on me?" He stood up.

"Please, sit down. I was trying to tell you what happened."

"You fucked another man! That's what happened!"

I started to whine. "Joann, please tell him to sit down so I can explain. Please."

Our counselor, Joann, spoke to Desmond. It took a while, but finally, he took a seat.

"I was in a dark place. I was feeling like I needed some excitement. I know it isn't an excuse for what I did, but he meant nothing. You mean everything. I was actually going to confess today. I love you, Desmond. I really do. And I'm sorry."

Tears fell from my eyes, but Desmond didn't see them. He had his back to me.

"Please forgive me. I want us. I want you. I love you so, so much. I've been trying to tell you. I just didn't know how. And then today, I told myself I was just going to tell you the truth."

Desmond shook his head. "I have never cheated on you. I never even thought about it. I love you that much. And for you..."

Desmond stood up again.

"Please sit down. Let's talk."

Desmond ignored me and walked towards the door.

I sobbed louder and louder until he disappeared.

I expected this reaction, but I was still angry with myself for bringing Tyrone into the picture in the first place. And I was mad as hell that Tyrone would tell Desmond after I've been fucking him for his silence the past few weeks.

With Desmond gone, the counselor and I had an honest, open conversation about what I needed and what I want. I told her everything that I couldn't say in front of Desmond, and she said things that I needed to hear.

One thing she did say was that if Desmond was at home when I got there, then we definitely had a chance to work things out. Sadly, he wasn't there when I arrived.

"Hey," Dejah greeted me.

"Hey."

She noticed my face. "Uh oh, Desmond found out about Tyrone, didn't he?"

I nodded and hung my head. "Tyrone told him! He fucking told Desmond!" I yelled.

"Are you surprised? He's a bum."

"And he has the audacity to still be calling me!" I pushed my ringing phone into Dejah's face, just before answering it.

"You a lame motherfucker! You told my husband! Really? Don't ever call me again! Ever!"

I hung up before Tyrone had a chance to say anything. He called back to back a few times until I blocked his number...again. And once I started to get calls from other random numbers, I sat there and changed my phone number altogether.

"Desmond will forgive you. He's a good guy. And he loves you and the kids. He'll forgive you."

"How can you be so sure?"

Dejah shrugged. "I'm not. But positive thoughts, okay?"

"I don't know, Dej. He was pissed. I mean, I have never seen him so upset before."

"And he has the right to be. Now, you just start kissing his ass. Jumping through every hoop possible. No matter what, you're at fault, so you have to do whatever you have to do to fix it."

After talking to Dejah and pretending to be okay in front of my kids, I made my way to the front porch. And I sat there. For hours. Waiting. Hoping. Praying that Desmond would just come home.

Finally, just before midnight, I headed inside.

Before showering, I grabbed the pregnancy test out of my purse that I'd been scared to take, and I peed on it.

I waited.

On pins and needles, I waited.

Suddenly, I heard my bedroom door open.

"Desmond?"

"What?" he growled.

Softly, I exhaled.

He came home.

My husband came home.

And glancing down at the pregnancy test, I smiled at the negative result before wrapping the test in toilet paper.

I'm not pregnant.

And my husband came home.

Goodbye, and good riddance lame ass Tyrone!

***

Chapter 4

"Tierra! You gotta' be kidding me right now!" Dejah stared at the ring on her finger.

"Nope! I'm married!"

Tierra squealed. The rest of us stared at her in concern.

"Damn, I expected a little more excitement," Tierra frowned.

"You have only known him a month, Tierra," Nicole finally spoke up.

"I know. But when you know...you just know."

"How can you know that you want to spend the rest of your life with someone after a month?" Dejah questioned. "It's impossible!"

Well, not really.

In just two short weeks, I knew that I wanted to marry Desmond someday. We were college kids, but I knew that he was everything I wanted in a man and that I wanted him to be my husband. Of course, we dated for a while before he popped the question, but had he asked me two weeks in, I would've said yes. And it seems like these days, I'm constantly being reminded of why I loved him so much, and I'm forced to realize how bad I messed things up.

Things between Desmond and I are bad.

Really bad.

We're arguing every day. He won't touch me. He barely even looks at me. And he keeps making me explain why I stepped out on him and our marriage, over and over again. As though he was trying to make it make sense.

But every single time, I told him the same thing. I explained. I cried. I did whatever I felt was necessary. I just didn't want him to leave me. But no matter what I said, it was never enough. I couldn't change what I did to him, and I couldn't take the pain away. I couldn't remove the pain from his face, his eyes, or out of his heart.

Before all of this, I'd only seen Desmond cry twice. Both times were happy tears. Once, at our wedding and the other time was during our first baby delivery.

But lately, he's been crying almost every day. And he would do it right in front of me. He wanted me to know how much I hurt him. And if I could do it all over again, I wouldn't make the same silly mistake.

"What's his favorite color?"

"Blue," Tierra answered.

"His favorite food?"

"Pasta."

"His favorite fruit?"

"Grapes," Tierra giggled. "Look, guys. I know it's sudden, but he's the one."

"Or is it that you were so desperate to find the one that you're forcing yourself to think that he is?" Dejah asked.

"Dej!" I scowled her.

"What? We were all thinking it. We all know that you've been a little desperate for love for a while now. We care about you. And we just want to make sure that you're going to be okay."

Tierra took a deep breath. "I'm going to be fine. Besides, all of you have your own problems to be worried about instead of worrying about me."

Now, all of the girls knew what Desmond and I were going through. And they knew that it was all my fault. And Dejah and her husband Tyree were still in a strange place. And of course, Nicole was still dealing with the drama surrounding David.

"Well, when will we get to meet him, at least?"

Tierra smiled. "Now."

We all turned around to see who Tierra was smiling at.

"Well, damn," Nicole mumbled.

A man who looked as though he was swallowed by muscles approached Tierra and hugged her.

"Ladies, this is Phillip."

"Hello, ladies. I've heard so much about you."

His smile was crooked, but his teeth were perfectly straight and pearly white. He was tanned, which probably came from hours of exercising outdoors, and he was somewhat short too. He and Tierra were the exact same height, but if I'm being honest, they did look good together. I couldn't stop staring at the vein in his forehead.

"This is my husband."

"Mr. Husband, don't you think a month of knowing someone is too soon to get married?" Dejah folded her arms across her chest.

"Typically, yes. But I fell in love with Tierra the same night we met. We're on the same page. We have so much in common. Why not marry the woman of my dreams?"

Tierra beamed.

She was happy.

And happiness looked good on her.

"Are you a psychopath?"

"No ma'am, I'm not."

"Do you like little girls?"

"Hell no! I don't."

"Are you gay?"

"Most definitely not."

He waited to see if we were going to ask him any other questions.

"Well, we're going to go," Tierra said. "I'll call you ladies later."

In silence, each of us stared at them until they disappeared.

"Steroids and dicks don't mix," Nicole said suddenly.

"What?" I laughed, and so did Dejah.

"He definitely takes steroids, and you know they say they make a man's dick small, or something like that. Good thing Tierra got all those damn toys. She's going to need them," Nicole howled in laughter.

We finished lunch, and once Dejah and I were inside my car, suddenly, she started to cry.

"I miss Tyree," she whined.

"Then go back home. Not that I don't love you and the kids being around, but if you miss your husband, go home."

Dejah continued to cry. "It's just…I know if I go back now, and if nothing changes, when I leave the next time…I'm done. And I'm just scared that we can't make things better."

"Trust me, as long as you haven't added anyone else into the mix, it's fixable. Start with dating each other and being friends again. See what happens from there."

I'd just given her the same advice the therapist gave me the day before when Desmond didn't show up for the second time.

"With everything going on with you and Desmond, I hate being in your space."

"I'm actually glad you guys are there. Things would probably be ten times worse."

We arrived at home, and my heart dropped into the pit of my stomach as Desmond loaded boxes in the back of his car.

Dejah headed inside as I headed towards Desmond.

"Hey, what are you doing?"

He didn't respond.

"Desmond? Are you…are you leaving me?"

Suddenly, he stopped moving.

Completely.

"Are you leaving me?" I repeated.

"I don't know," he managed to say. And then he looked at me. "I just know that I can't be in this house with you and figure it out."

"Please, please don't go. I'm sorry about Tyrone. I'll never do it again. Just please don't go."

I sobbed. I was trying not to. I was trying to be strong, but I was losing my husband, and there was nothing that I could do about it.

"I just need some time. I'll be at my brother's house."

Desmond slammed the trunk closed, and with me standing there with a face full of tears, my husband drove away from me.

My marriage is over.

***

"You and that baby can go to hell!"

The lady shouted at Nicole just as I approached her.

"Whoa, what's going on here?"

Nicole called me at work. She said no one else was answering their phones, and she asked me to come by her house. She told me that David had come by and that a woman had followed him there. Glancing down at her ring finger, this woman must be his wife.

She and Nicole were complete opposites, physically, but she was gorgeous. She wasn't as shapely as Nicole. She had titties the size of cantaloupes and barely even a scoop of ass, but the features of her face and her skin were both a sight to see.

"Once you knew for sure he was married, that should've been it!"

"He's the one over here bothering me! Not the other way around. I've been trying to cut him off and distance myself from him. He won't leave me alone!"

"Don't lie! I've read some of your text messages back and forth recently. You still want him. But you can't have him. Unless you don't mind having him broke! Because I'm going to take him for every penny he has if he leaves me!"

I studied Nicole's facial expression. She seemed sad. Miserable even. And I wished that I could help her in some way.

"As I said, he won't stop bothering me. I don't want him. I don't even want this baby I'm having by him."

"Well, you should do your research before letting a man into your bed! Some dogs with collars are still strays. And some men who don't wear their wedding ring are still married!"

"Hell, he was taking my out of town and all out in the open..."

"He had to take you out of town because he has a wife! Duh! He told me they were business trips. He's a liar! The difference between us is that this liar belongs to me!"

David hadn't said a word since I'd arrived.

"You should be ashamed of yourself! You're a married man, with a baby on the way by someone else, and all of these other women on the side. And now, you have your wife and the mother of your unborn child, standing outside, arguing because you won't keep your ass at home! Get your shit together! And leave my friend alone!"

David didn't respond. His wife started to yell at him again, and eventually, he just walked away with her still screaming behind him.

"I swear I haven't been talking to him...lately."

"Girl, you don't have to explain nothing to me. All of this is his fault. Not yours. You just continue to rest. You have to be strong for this baby. You shouldn't even be on your feet right now. Come on, let's get you inside."

"How in the hell did they end up over here anyway?"

"I guess she followed him. I didn't know he was coming here. The last thing I said to him was to never call me again, and then he shows up here, with his wife not too far behind him. Now, she knows where I live."

"Good. Maybe now he will stay the hell away from you." I helped Nicole put her feet up.

"This is all too much."

"I know this probably makes you feel some kind of way. Considering what ole' boy did. I can't believe he told Desmond."

"Girl, don't even get me started!"

Needless to say, I never made it back to work.

I sat with Nicole for hours. We talked and laughed. I cooked for her. I was even prepared to stay over, but she told me she would be fine. As soon as I was outside, I called my husband.

Whenever we talk, since he left the house, Desmond and I mostly argue. Simple conversations usually end with him asking me something random about Tyrone. And if he doesn't get the response that he was looking for, even if it's the truth, Desmond gets upset, and we end up arguing like cats and dogs for hours.

"Hello?"

I exhaled. "Hey."

"Hey."

"Um, what are you doing?"

Desmond was quiet. After about a minute of silence, he finally spoke.

"I have to go meet Taylor."

"Taylor? The woman that you work with? Whose perfume you smelled like that day?"

"Yes."

"Why?" My heart skipped a beat.

"Why what?"

"Why are you meeting her?"

"Does it matter? It's work-related.

I didn't believe him.

Was Desmond going to cheat on me because I cheated on him? It had crossed my mind a few times. It was something that I probably would've done if the shoe was on the other foot.

"Do you remember your vows?" Desmond interrupted my thoughts.

"Of course."

"Tell me," he said.

"Tell you what?"

"Tell me your vows. Tell me what you said to me that day, in a church full of our family and friends. Tell me what you said to me."

I remembered my vows word for word because I'd memorized them for a whole week before my wedding day. Everyone told me to just speak from the heart that day, but I wanted to make sure that I told him how much he meant to me and exactly what I felt about him, so I wrote them down, from my heart, and memorized them.

The funny thing is, after the wedding, Desmond admitted to doing the same thing. He said he hadn't wanted to forget anything, so he wrote everything down that he'd wanted to say.

"Tell me," Desmond repeated.

"I vow to love you, always. I vow to never give up on you. To never give up on us. I'll show up to the fight of life with you, every single day. As long as we're together, no matter what, we'll always make a way. You are everything I want. You're everything I needed. And I vow to be yours and only yours until the end of time. I am yours. Forever. For always. And you are mine."

I exhaled. I wanted to cry, but I didn't. I just held the phone with a tight grip as I waited for Desmond's next words.

"You said that you vow to be mine and only mine, until the end of time. That's what you said."

"And I meant it. I really did. And I still do."

Desmond was quiet again. "The last sentence of my vows was..."

"You can count on me. Forever. I'll never give up on you, and I'll never stop loving you." I finished his sentence.

"So, don't give up on me. Don't give up on us. Keep your vows."

"Did you keep yours?" Desmond snapped on me.

"Not entirely. But two wrongs don't make a right, baby. I'm just asking for another chance to get our vows right this time. I'm asking you not to give up on us."

It seems as though I was begging and pleading with him every day, but I didn't care. Whatever I had to do to get him to come back home to me, I would.

"Can I come and get the kids Friday."

"You don't ever have to ask that, Desmond."

"Okay," he said and hung up without saying goodbye.

I swear, if I get my husband back, I'm never cheating again! I don't even want to look at another man.

For the rest of the drive home, I thought of things I could say and do that might bring Desmond back home to me.

***

"Michael is on line one."

"Hey, Michael," I said, placing the phone to my ear.

"Hello, boss lady. I just wanted to run a few things by you. I think they may be things to get to the editor, but I wanted your personal opinion, if that's okay."

"Sure. I have some time. Run it by me."

For the next hour or so, Michael and I discussed books and business. He had an accent. He was born and raised in the Bronx, and I loved the way he talked. And he was very intelligent too. He used big words and actually used them correctly in a sentence.

"I won't take up any more of your time," he said. "And tell your husband that I'm in line. I'm waiting."

"Excuse me?"

Michael chuckled. "I overheard you and your assistant talking last week when I came by the office. You said he was leaving you. I'm sorry you're going through that. I've been there. Divorce is no joke; I'll tell you that. But if you guys don't reconcile things...I'm in line. And I'm waiting."

Michael hung up after he clearly came on to me. And I'm glad he did because I had no idea how to respond to him. Michael reminded me of my husband. A lot. He's sexy. Bold. Smart and ambitious.

But I don't want Michael. I don't want Tyrone. Or any other man for that matter.

I want Desmond.

I want my husband back.

With him on my mind, I decided to call him.

"Sir, I said you can't go in there. Sir!"

Tyrone stormed into my office.

"I'm so sorry. I tried to stop him."

"It's okay, Sage."

My assistant rolled her eyes at Tyrone before walking out of my office and closing the door behind her.

"What the fuck do you want?" I growled.

"You."

I huffed. "Tyrone, please, just get the hell out of my office! I swear you were the biggest mistake of my life!"

"Nah, I doubt that," Tyrone took a seat. "But if you keep tripping, I might become your biggest problem, though."

Tyrone glared at me.

"What? What don't you get? Whatever we had going on is over! What are you? Some kind of stalker or something? Someone who doesn't like to take no for an answer?"

"I've been told that a time or two," Tyrone relaxed. "So, you think you get to just come into my world, let me fuck the shit out of you as much as I want to, and then just cut me off because all of a sudden you wanna' be a good wife?"

"Uh, yeah. I was going through something. You scratched the itch. What do you want me to say? Thank you? Fine, I'll say thank you. Thank you, Tyrone, for giving me some dick when I wasn't getting pleased at home. But it was a mistake. You already told my husband and ruined my marriage, so just leave."

"Well, if your marriage is over…what's stopping us from fucking all over this desk right now?"

Previously, comments like that, from him, would've turned me on.

Not anymore.

"I wouldn't have sex with you again to save my life. Now, leave."

Tyrone stared at me for a while.

"I said…leave!"

Finally, he stood up.

"I want what I want. And I always get what I want. So, either you stop being a bitch and give it to me. Or…I'm just going to have to take it," Tyrone threatened me with a smile. "I don't wanna be ya' man. I just wanna keep fuckin' ya' every now and then. See you around, Bailey."

I held my breath until he was out of sight.

I shook my head in pure disgust.

Leave it to me to go out and have an affair with a damn psychopath!

"Knock, knock," my assistant, Sage, came back into my office. "Is everything okay?"

Sage was my new assistant. She's only been working for me for about six months. She's a sweet girl, but she's about ten years younger than me, so even though we chatted sometimes, I wouldn't call us friends. She only knows about me and Desmond splitting up because I was an emotional wreck at work and started crying one day. She was there, so I decided to vent to her, though I didn't tell her that I was the cause of our problems or about my affair.

"Yes, I'm okay. I love that dress!" I said in an attempt to seem fine.

"Thank you, boss lady," Sage said, shutting my office door behind her.

I thought about Tyrone's words.

And I thought about his behavior too.

He always seemed a little possessive, but never to this extent.

All I know is he's not going to make me have sex with him, no matter what he says.

He was a mistake.

And a mistake that I never plan to make again.

***

"How do I look?"

"So pretty, mommy!" My daughter squealed.

"You look good," Dejah smiled. "I would hit that," she laughed.

"Shut up."

Two weeks after he left, finally, Desmond agreed to go to dinner with me.

"Get your husband back tonight, girl. Do you hear me?"

"I'm going to try my best."

"No, don't try. Do. Hell, pull out all your bag of tricks. He obviously still loves you or he wouldn't even be going out with you. Everything is going to be fine."

Dejah watched me walk to my car, and I got inside, nervous as ever as though I was going on a blind date.

We were meeting at Desmond's favorite French restaurant, and I rehearsed what I wanted to say to him over and over again the whole ride there.

He was waiting for me by the entrance when I arrived.

"I'm getting my husband back tonight," I mumbled as I walked towards him. "I'm getting my husband back tonight."

"Hi."

"Hi."

Desmond looked good and smelled even better as he held the door open for me to go inside.

Here goes nothing.

"Desmond..." I started to say once we were seated.

"Look, tonight, let's not talk about...it. Let's just try to have dinner. Okay?"

Sure enough, I was about to apologize for my infidelity for the 1000th time, but per his request, I simply nodded my head instead.

"So, uh, how is work?"

"Work is good. I'm coming up for a promotion."

"Really? What? Is Richard or Kenneth retiring or something?" I inquired about the only two men in higher positions than him at the company.

"No. Actually, it's to run another office that's being opened...in D.C."

"D.C.? As in Washington, D.C.?" I swallowed the lump in my throat.

"Yes."

"And you're not going to take it, right? The kids need you. I need you," I admitted.

Desmond cleared his throat. "Well, if we get a divorce..."

"We're not getting a divorce!" I slammed my hand down against the table. Other customers looked in our direction as the waiter came over and started to ask questions. Once we ordered a few drinks, Desmond sat quietly, waiting for me to say the first words.

"As you said, we're not talking about any of that tonight, okay? Let's just talk about something else."

Desmond exhaled. "Well, I guess I should start by saying that your booty is about to pop out of that dress. Damn girl, it seems as though you've gained about ten pounds in the ass."

I chuckled.

The mood was changed.

And for the next few minutes, we managed to laugh and joke with each other. And it felt good. It felt like the old times. It felt like the old us. The part of us that I so desperately wanted back.

"Do you remember the first night we moved into our house?"

"Do I? You mean when you thought the previous owners somehow had cameras all over the house watching us?" Desmond laughed.

"I swear it felt like someone was watching us. I wasn't being paranoid."

"Yes, you were."

"Well, you took it all away by making a joke out of it and suggesting that we had sex in every room of the house just to give them a show. And we did just that."

"Yes. We did."

Desmond took a sip of his drink, and flirtatiously, I took a sip of mine. Suddenly, I got an idea. I was willing to do just about anything to get him to see that I made a terrible mistake and that I wanted another chance.

"Make love to me tonight, Desmond."

"What?"

"You heard me. I'm done eating. You're done eating. And I have something else that you can eat. All night long."

Desmond tugged at his blazer.

"It doesn't have to mean anything if you don't want it to. I just need you. I need to feel you. I want you. Do you want me?"

"I never stopped wanting you."

"Well..."

I stood up, allowing him to get an eye full of my booty.

"Then come get me. Pay the check. I'll be waiting outside."

I sashayed away, slowly, hoping that he was watching. I held my breath until I was outside.

"Bailey," I spoke to myself as I walked towards my car. "Tonight, you gotta' fuck him like never before. Take his soul, girl. Take his soul!"

Once inside my car, I waited for Desmond to come outside. Once he appeared, I drove towards him.

"Bailey...I just don't think..." Desmond said once he was inside of his car.

I shook my head and sped into the parking space beside him.

After getting out of my car, I waited for him to unlock the passenger side door.

"Bailey..."

"Ssshh..."

He may not be ready to have sex with me, but I could give him a little something to remind him of what he's missing.

"Stop, what are you doing?" Desmond asked as I tugged at his zipper.

"Ssshhh..."

"Bailey, no," Desmond said just as I grabbed his dick. His mouth was saying no, but his nine inches of dick was rock hard and screaming yes.

"I just want to make you feel good. Let me make you feel good," I whispered just before shoving his dick into my mouth.

Desmond continued to act as though he wanted me to stop, but it didn't take long for his demands to stop became long, low moans.

I slurped and sucked like never before. I gave him the best head in the history of sucking dick. I'm sure of it.

It didn't take him long to release himself.

There was an awkward silence between us as we both got ourselves together.

"Ummm...I guess call me," I said to Desmond.

He didn't respond.

In a weird way, he seemed upset.

I opened his car door, and as soon as I shut the passenger side door, he sped off without even saying goodbye.

"Damn!"

Getting back into my car, I called him, but he didn't answer his phone.

What's the problem?

I called Desmond a few more times, and finally, frustrated, I drove myself to the bar.

"Vodka, no ice."

"Someone must've had a bad date," I heard his voice behind me.

Tyrone.

"What? How do you know I was on a date?"

"How do you think I know?"

He smiled and sat down beside me.

"Tyrone, I'm not in the mood, okay? Please just leave me alone."

"Yeah, see, the problem is, I don't want to."

"So, what, you're just going to follow me around? Stalk me? What do I have to do, take out a restraining order on you to keep you away from me?" I gulped down another shot of vodka. "I'm sure you don't need any more charges. Let's just call it what it was and move on."

"Like I said, I move on when I want to move on. Not when some trick is ready to move on."

"Trick?"

"Married Trick," he corrected himself and grabbed my arm.

I stood to my feet.

"Let go of me! You know what…"

"Bailey?" I heard a voice behind me. "Is everything alright?"

Michael.

I was surprised and happy to see him at the same time.

"Yes, everything is fine," I lied.

"Bro, you can move on. Mind your business," Tyrone growled.

"Or what?" Michael stood close to me. "Bailey, what are you drinking? Next round is on me," Michael helped me on the stool.

After staring at us in anger for a few seconds, finally, Tyrone stood up.

I noticed a few of his friends not too far away, and suddenly, I became worried about Michael. I wasn't sure if Tyrone would start a fight that would lead to Michael being hurt, or worse, but luckily, Tyrone didn't say anything else.

He simply walked away.

"Who was that?" Michael asked immediately.

"A bad, bad mistake," I admitted.

"Oh."

Michael didn't ask anything else about Tyrone. And for a little while, we drank and laughed and talked about everything from books, to what retirement looked like for each of us.

By the time we walked out of the bar, I was way passed my limit, so Michael suggested that I leave my car overnight and called me a cab.

"You could've taken me home, you know," I tapped Michael's bottom lip with my index finger. "Or you could've just taken me to your place."

Why the hell did I just say that?

I shook my head.

"Yeah, the way you're looking in that dress. It's just better to call you a cab," Michael smiled at me.

The cab finally arrived.

"Take care, boss," he said once he made sure the driver had my address and that I was comfortable in the backseat.

"Bye, Michael," I sang out the window like a five-year-old as the cab started to drive away.

The cool night air attempted to sober me up, but I knew that it was going to take a hot shower and at least eight hours of sleep to get me where I needed to be.

"Thank you, sir," I slurred, reaching the cab driver too much money just before slamming the cab door shut.

He sped away as I looked for my keys in my purse.

And then, suddenly, bright lights came out of nowhere, and I heard the truck hit the brakes.

It all happened so fast.

Tyrone put his hands around my mouth, pulled me to his truck, and threw me inside.

He sped away chuckling as I punched at him, but he didn't stop driving.

Aww, hell!

***

"Ma'am, you said you want to press charges?"

The cop spoke loudly.

"No...no. Nevermind."

I ran out of the police department in tears.

Tyrone raped me.

He literally threw me in his car, drove me a block or two from my house, pulled over behind a building, held me down, and raped me.

I was so drunk and dizzy, but I tried my best to fight him off. I fought him as best as I could. I even started to cry, but he didn't care. He held me down and took what he wanted from me. And with me covered in tears and vomit, he drove me back home and said he had plenty of proof that would show that he and I were having an affair and that the cops wouldn't believe me.

I was in shock. Disbelief that Tyrone would go that far.

I sat outside on my front porch all night in tears and then had Dejah to take me to get my car once she saw me sitting on the porch.

She thought I had a bad date with Desmond. She asked me questions over and over again, but I didn't answer her. Once I was in my car, I drove myself to the police station to press charges on Tyrone. It took me forever to get up the courage to get out of my car, and now, I can't force myself to do what I came here for.

"Shit!" I screamed back inside my car.

What if Tyrone is right?

What if the police don't believe me?

I thought about all the nasty text messages and pictures that we'd exchanged in the past. I wondered if he could call me a liar and actually get away with what he did to me.

My phone started to vibrate in my lap.

Desmond.

For the first time, since he left, I wasn't in a hurry to answer his call. In all honesty, I wasn't in the right headspace to talk to him, but I answered my phone anyway.

"Hello?"

"I came by the house last night after leaving the way that I did. You weren't there."

He came by?

I regretted not going straight home after the restaurant. None of this would've happened if I'd just gone home.

"I'm sorry for just driving off like that. I was an asshole. I know you're trying. And having you right there, sucking my dick, just reminded me of how much I missed you. And then I thought about what you did to put us in this situation. Either way, it's no excuse for leaving you out there like that. And I apologize."

I didn't say anything.

"Bailey?"

I tried to hold back the tears, but I couldn't. I started to cry, and once I started, I couldn't stop. I could hear Desmond apologizing over and over again, thinking that he was the cause of my tears.

"Bailey? I wasn't trying to be disrespectful."

"Desmond..." I sobbed, but that I was all I could say. I ended up hanging up the phone on him, and for two hours, in the parking lot at the police station, I sat there and cried more than I'd ever cried before.

It was like freshman year in college all over again.

Freshman year of college, I was a wild one.

I was going to all the parties. I was drinking, and I was having sex with whoever I felt like having sex with at the time. I'll be the first to admit that I was doing a little too much, but no still means no...right?

Rodney Hall.

That was his name.

We'd flirted a few times, but he had a girlfriend at the time. That night, I saw him at the party. I could tell that he wanted me. He followed me around all night. He kept offering me drinks. And he couldn't seem to keep his hands off me, but I was actually hoping to hook up with someone else. Yet, as the night went on, I drunk more and more, and I found myself laid across some random person's bed. I just needed to close my eyes for a second. I was trying to sober up. And then, Rodney came into the room.

At first, he just talked to me. We even laughed a little, and he pretended to be as drunk as I was. At first, he kept touching my face and my hair. And then he started to rub all over me. I kept moving his hands, but soon, he got more aggressive.

I told him no.

Several times.

I told him I didn't want to have sex with him. I even got off the bed and attempted to leave the room, but he pushed me back onto the bed. I remember the smell of his breath and him holding my arms down and telling me how beautiful I was. I remember him telling me how bad he wanted me and that in his mind, he already felt like I wanted him too.

Long story short...Rodney raped me too.

And I was too drunk to fight him off. I felt numb as he pumped away on top of me. And I remember him kissing me on the cheek once he was done and saying thank you.

And then he left me there. Panties ripped off, throwing up on the floor. And the soberer I became, the more it started to set in what had happened to me.

At the time, I was too embarrassed to tell anyone.

I surely was embarrassed to go to the police.

So, I said nothing.

I didn't tell a soul.

Anytime I saw him, I damn near ran in the opposite direction. He never said another word to me, either. Never tried to apologize. There was nothing he could say that could change what he did to me.

In a way, he changed me. Well, the situation did. I got more focused on my studies. I changed the way I looked at life. And for the rest of my college years, I never drunk again. I didn't even date anyone again, or even wanted to, until I met Desmond my senior year.

I couldn't believe something like that had happened to me. And now it has happened again.

And though I'm embarrassed, this time, I just wonder if something will actually be done about it. If the police will believe me over Tyrone. If he would be able to call me a liar and if they will think I'm just angry at him and trying to get him in trouble, versus believing that I was actually telling the truth.

If...

I continued to cry harder and harder as my thoughts taunted me.

My life is so fucked up!

This can't be my life!
It just can't be!

***

Chapter 5

"Uh-huh," Dejah cleared her throat. "I'm waiting."

I exhaled loudly.

"Tell me, Bailey."

"Tell you what?"

"Something is off about you. I'm not stupid. So, I'm waiting for you to tell me."

I never told her about what happened to me in college. I never told anyone. I just pretended as though it never happened.

"Dejah…"

"Spill it!"

I took a deep breath. "Tyrone…"

"Oh, hell no! I thought you were done with him?"

"He…"

"What?"

"If you shut up and let me get it out, I'll tell you," I mumbled.

"Sorry."

"The other night…Tyrone…raped me, Dej," I whispered.

She looked at me confused. After reading my facial expression, she knew that I was serious.

"How…what…. what the fuck!"

"Ssshh!" I patted her leg.

"Are you serious, right now, Bailey?"

I nodded.

"We have to go to the police! Are you okay? I'm sorry, Bailey," Dejah managed to get out between deep breaths.

"I tried to go to the police. I left. I didn't know if they would believe me. I didn't know if they would think it's all my fault. I just want to forget it ever happened."

"Fuck that! He needs to go to jail!"

Tyrone raped me four days ago, and I've blocked at least ten different phone numbers from him calling my phone as though he didn't do anything.

He could care less about what he did to me.

It was as though he was a monster.

I can't believe that I didn't see all of this in him before. If I had, I would've never, ever, let him touch me.

I won't call this karma because what he did to me was sick! But I will say that I'm definitely paying for the bad decisions that I made. And I wish I could take it all back. I wish I'd never said a word back to Tyrone that night.

"You have to tell the police! Did you tell Desmond?"

"No!" I yelled at her. "I don't want him to know about this. Ever. That's why I'm just going to let it go and move on with my life."

"Let it go?" Dejah said in disbelief. "How can you even say that? How can you just let something like this go? And what if he does it again? To you? To someone else?"

"Dejah…I just want to forget about it, okay. I just want to forget about Tyrone. And the past few months. I just want my life back. I want my husband back. My family back." I started to cry.

My phone started to vibrate in my hand.

It was an unknown number.

"Just leave me alone. Just leave me alone," I shook my head.

"Who is that? Huh? Is that him?"

Dejah snatched my phone out of my hand.

"Listen here, you trifling, rapist motherfucker!" Dejah screamed as she answered the phone. "Uh, oh, oooh, um, sorry, Mrs. Williams."

My eyes grew as big as golf balls.

Dejah reached for my cellphone in shame.

"Hello, Ma," I spoke. "Oh, no, Dejah's crazy self is always doing or saying something random. You know how she is." I tried to cover up Dejah's comments. "Ma, why are you calling me from an unknown number?"

I listened to what my mother had to say, and a few minutes later, she hung up the phone.

"Sorry," Dejah shrugged. "But we have to do something."

"There's nothing to do. I didn't go to the police. I just want him to go away. I just want him to leave me alone."

"You have to stand up to him, or he's never going to stop! At this point, he's just doing whatever the fuck he wants to do to you! He ruined your marriage. He raped you. What else are you going to let him do?"

Dejah was so upset that she ended up stepping outside.

I sat there, watching random numbers call my phone over and over again. I had no idea as to how Tyrone had gotten my new number in the first place, but I refused to talk to him.

He was becoming my worst nightmare, and I was waiting for someone to wake me up.

Come on, Bailey. Just wake up.

***

"Moving?"
Tierra smiled.
"Yes. Next month."
We were having our weekly girl's lunch, and Tierra was glowing like never before. Her hair was different, she was wearing make-up, and she was even dressed up. We were all so used to seeing her in black all the time, since she's a hairstylist, but not today. She was showing some skin, wearing some color, and I couldn't do a thing but smile at her.

"We're moving to Las Vegas."
"Las Vegas!" Dejah yelled.

"Yes! My hubby is opening a brand-new gym there. He said that it's always been his dream. So, I'm moving."

"Tierra. Wait, wait, wait. Now, come on. You just married the man. And now you're moving away? Tierra, it's too fast. It's all too fast. It just doesn't make sense."

"Dejah, look…"

"Can I come?" Nicole interrupted.

All eyes were suddenly on her.

"What?"

"I said, can I come? To Las Vegas with y'all? I have about $25,000 saved up. I'll find a job after I have the baby. I just…I just want to go."

Tierra touched her hand. "Yes. You can come. You can stay with us. We already have a four-bedroom house waiting for us. You and the baby are welcome to stay as long as you need to."

"Wait, both of y'all bitches talking about leaving us? Seriously?"

"I'll follow my husband to the end of the world," Tierra smiled.

"I just need to get the fuck away from here," Nicole growled. "And away from David. The sooner, the better."

I wish I could just pick up and move. Maybe I wouldn't feel like I was suffocating.

If I didn't have my company, maybe getting Desmond to take that job in D.C. and taking us with him wouldn't be such a bad idea.

"Bailey? Nothing to say?"

"No. I wish you both nothing the best. You both deserve nothing but happiness."

"What? Don't listen to Bailey! She got her own shit going on right now. Both of you need to stay y'all assess right here!" Dejah pouted.

"Aww, you're going to miss us?"

"Hell yeah. I'm not going to deny it," Dejah shrugged. "So, stay."

The girls started to talk back and forth, and then I heard my name.

"Hello, Bailey."

His voice made my skin crawl.

"Get the fuck away from this goddamn table before I call the police!" Dejah yelled.

I was frozen. Literally. I couldn't move. I couldn't speak. I couldn't do anything.

"Who is this?" Nicole asked.

"The guy," Tierra whispered. "The "other" guy."

"Oh, the man Bailey cheated on Desmond with? Ooooh, damn," she said, studying Tyrone.

"Ooooh, nothing! He's a goddamn rapist!" Dejah blurted out, completely embarrassing me since I hadn't told the other ladies. "Now, you get your goddamn ass away from this table or so help me God…"

"Chill, little mama. I'm out. I'll see you later, Bailey," he said.

I didn't look at him.

"Oh, no the fuck you won't!" Dejah yelled behind him.

Once I figured he was far enough away, I started to pant.

"I can't breathe. I can't breathe."

The ladies surrounded me and tried to help me catch my breath.

"It's okay, Bailey. It's okay."

"No. It's not. It's just not." Finally able to breathe, I started to cry.

"What's this about rape?" Tierra asked.

"Nothing."

"Nothing, my ass! Did Tyrone rape you? When?"

"Please, Tierra. Please."

The ladies respected my wishes and left the topic alone, but I knew that they were going to want details sooner or later, thanks to Dejah's big mouth.

The rest of lunch was awkward. No one really knew what to say. Shortly afterward, we all left and went our separate ways.

I drove towards the highway, and completely lost in my thoughts, I found myself an hour away from home. Only then did I notice Tyrone's truck following behind me in my rearview mirror.

He's relentless.

Pure evil.

He literally has nothing better to do other than follow me around and make my life pure hell.

I stopped at a gas station.

I went inside the store, and shortly after, in came Tyrone.

"Stop following me! Leave me alone!"

Tyrone grinned. "Stop acting like that."

"Acting? You think this is a joke? Do you think I'm playing with you?"

Tyrone opened one of the freezers and got himself a soda. "You're the one making this harder than it has to be. Stop acting stupid. Let's get back on good terms. Problem solved."

"Never! I'll die before I let you touch me again." I noticed people staring at us. "This man is a rapist. He raped me, and now he's stalking me!" I was so furious, and I couldn't believe I'd said the words aloud, but I had.

Tyrone stared at me as though he wanted to choke me.

"Ma'am, are you okay? Is this man bothering you?"

"Yes, sir. He is! He's stalking me."

"Sir, I'm going to have to ask you to leave the store and the premises. Or I'll be forced to call the police."

I could tell that Tyrone was embarrassed, but he kept a grin on his face.

"Sir…"

"I'm leaving. I'll see you later. You have to come back home," Tyrone said to me. And after dropping the bottle of soda on the floor, he walked out of the store.

Once he was gone, the owner asked if I needed the police, but I told him I was okay.

That was the lie of the century.

I wasn't okay.

I was far from okay.

The look in Tyrone's eyes told me that he was getting off on making my life hell. And he had no intentions of leaving me alone anytime soon.

From the looks of it, there's only one way to get rid of him...kill him.

Okay, not really. But what else am I supposed to do?

***

"Are you okay?"

"Yes. Why do you ask that?"

Michael sat back in his chair.

"For starters, it's all over your face."

We were having a meeting to talk more about some changes to his new book. He was very hands-on, full of ideas. I liked that. He was the gem that was going to bring my publishing company even more recognition.

"I'm fine."

"Or, you could be honest and say that you're not. I've been told that I'm a pretty good listener."

Michael smiled at me.

"I'll be okay. Really. So, let's talk about this chapter."

"Fuck that chapter. Come on."

"What?"

Michael stood up in from his chair and came around my desk.

"Come on," he said, reaching out his hand.

"Where are we going?"

Michael grabbed my hand and told me to grab my purse. I told my assistant that we would be back shortly.

Once we were outside, I was surprised to see that he drove a Range Rover. I realized then that I'd never asked him what he did outside of writing.

"Nice ride."

"Thanks," he held open the door for me to get inside of his car.

"Book sales on your own must be pretty good."

"They are. But my IT company brings in a pretty penny too."

Oooh! A writer and an entrepreneur.

Michael refused to tell me where we were going. We talked the entire ride. He cracked jokes and made me laugh. I could tell that he was trying to cheer me up.

I appreciated it.

"Hmmm, what's this spot? I don't think I've ever been here."

"It's Heaven on Earth…seriously, that's the name of it. It's a Jamaican spot."

"I love Jamaican food."

Michael smiled as we walked inside.

To my surprise, it was more than a restaurant. There was a stage, a live band, and a dance floor. The dance floor was crowded with people, although it was only two o'clock in the afternoon.

The whole vibe was relaxing, almost soothing to the soul. Indoor palm trees, ceiling fans, comfortable sitting.

Michael found us a table, and after ordering, he asked me to dance.

"Uh, I don't know…"

"Come on," he smiled.

We joined the other people on the dance floor, and Michael started to show off his moves.

"Okay, then, just keep on surprising me today, why don't you."

Michael chuckled. "I'm a man of many, many talents." He grabbed my hands, and together, we started to sway to the beat. I found myself lost in the music. All of my worries about my marriage and Tyrone were gone. I finally felt good. I felt free.

I enjoyed myself so much that two hours later, I still didn't want to leave.

"Thank you," I said to Michael once we arrived back at the office. "I really needed that. I really, really did."

"It was my pleasure."

Though I knew it was totally inappropriate, I kissed his cheek before telling him to come back tomorrow so we could actually get some work done on his book. I stood on the sidewalk as he drove away and until his car was out of sight.

"New man?"

I heard behind me.

Desmond. He startled me.

"No. Actually, he really is one of my new authors."

"You kiss all of your authors?"

"Most of them," I lied, in hopes of making the kiss seem as innocent as possible to my husband. "He realized how down I was about you and took me to lunch. He's married. There's nothing for you to be concerned about."

I was hoping that my lies wouldn't catch up with me again, but I didn't want to give Desmond any more doubts than he already had.

"The only person that I want to kiss, in that way, is you," I walked closer to him. "What are you doing anyway?"

I could tell that my nonchalant approach about Michael was making him second guess how he'd initially planned to react towards me.

"I just came by. To check on you. You've been really down lately. In a different way. Something doesn't seem right. And I just wanted to check on you. That's all. But I guess ole' boy had it covered."

"Nope, not even a little bit," I pulled Desmond by the hand inside the building and into my office.

"I miss you," I said to him. "And I want you to come home."

"I want to come home."

My eyes lit up as bright as the star on top of a Christmas tree.

"But I can't. Not yet. If we're ever going to get back together, it's going to take a lot of talking. A lot of counseling. A lot of learning how to trust again."

"I'll do whatever you want and need me to do."

"Anything?"

"Yes, anything. I'll do anything to save my marriage. Anything to get you back and to have my family whole again."

"Bend that ass over on the desk then."

His comment caught me off guard. His comment actually reminded me of Tyrone...which didn't turn me on at all.

"Oh, so I'm not the only thing you miss, huh?"

I tried to play off how disturbed I was feeling. My husband finally wants to have sex with me, so I have to do this. And I can't let him know that something is wrong.

I kissed Desmond, and after a minute or so of fondling each other, I turned around and bent over my desk just as he'd asked.

***

"So, how is everything going?"

"Uhhh," Dejah started. "It's going. I guess. Tyree is still looking for work, so he seems super stressed. But he says he's happy that we're back home. I guess we'll see how everything goes. Why? You miss me here, don't you?"

"Bitch, don't nobody miss you," I smiled.

"Uh-huh. Don't worry. Your hubby will be home soon. Since y'all doing the nasty in your office and shit."

Since having sex with Desmond in my office, things had definitely picked up. We were talking a lot more, and finally, he was ready to go back to a counseling session with me.

"Should I tell him about…"

"Hell no. Hell no. And hell no again. Unless you're going to do something about it, then what's the point?"

"He's my husband. He should know that Tyrone…"

"And so should the cops. But you won't go press charges. So, here we are. Look, your marriage is already hanging by a thread. Imagine what damage telling him that is going to cause. And not to mention, Desmond is going to want to do something about it. Whether he wants to go to the police or beat Tyrone's ass, he's not just going to let that go or let it ride. He's going to want to do something. So, if you tell him, just be ready for that."

She's right.

Desmond wouldn't just let something like that go.

"Look, friend, what Tyrone did was fucked up. I want to kill him myself. But unless you are going to go through with pressing charges that now will probably be hell trying to prove, I wouldn't tell Desmond."

I hung out with Dejah for a while, and then a surprise text message from Desmond asking to come over, cut our visit short, and I rushed to try to get cute.

He said he was coming to see the kids, but I knew that he wanted to see me too. Just as Desmond pulled into the yard, my cell phone started to go crazy with back to back calls from unknown numbers.

"Hello, beautiful," Desmond said as soon as I opened the front door.

Just then, a car horn sounded, causing us both to look in that direction.

"Damn, baby, why aren't you answering the phone? I've been calling you all day," Tyrone said, hanging out of the truck window.

Desmond looked at me.

"No. It's not what you think. I swear."

Tyrone beeped his horn again.

"I swear to God, if you don't leave and leave me alone, I will go to the police about what you did! Get the fuck away from my house, Tyrone!"

Tyrone chuckled. "See you soon, Bailey."

He sped away, and immediately, I tried to explain to Desmond.

"I swear, he's stalking me. I don't talk to him. I don't fool around with him. Look. Look at all these missed calls from unknown numbers. He keeps calling and showing up. I swear. I swear Desmond, please believe me."

I wanted to cry, but I didn't.

"What did you mean go to the police about what he did?" Desmond asked.

"What?"

"You said you would go to the police about what he didn't if he didn't leave. What did he do?"

I didn't know whether to lie or tell the truth. All I knew was that Tyrone was getting out of control, and he was going to keep trying to ruin my life unless I stopped him.

I stepped onto the front porch and closed the door behind me.

"The night…that you and I went out. Tyrone followed me. I went to a bar, and when I got home, I was drunk. Tyrone grabbed me before I could make it inside the house, put me in his truck, drove me somewhere, and forced himself on me. He raped me."

Anger immediately consumed Desmond's face.

"That next morning, I went to the police station. I was going to press charges against him, but I just didn't. Since we'd had an affair, I didn't think they would believe me.

And I thought that after doing something like that I would never have to see Tyrone again, and I could just try to forget about it, but he acts as though he couldn't care less about what he did. He won't stop calling. He won't stop following me. He won't stop popping up. He was the biggest mistake of my life, and I'm so sorry. I'm sorry that I brought him into our marriage. I'm so sorry, Desmond."

I couldn't hold back my tears.

I started to cry, but Desmond didn't hold me.

"He did what to you?"

"He raped me, Desmond. He raped me."

Desmond yelled in frustration. "I'm going to kill him!"

"No. Our kids need you. I need you."

"I'm your husband, Bailey! I'm still your goddamn husband! So, what am I supposed to do? Let him get away with doing something like that to you? Tell me, what am I supposed to do?"

"I don't know, Desmond! I don't know!"

I sobbed loud and hard. Finally, Desmond walked closer to me and pulled me into his arms.

"I fucked everything up, and I'm so sorry. I'm so sorry."

Desmond didn't say a word. He just stood there, holding me, lost in his thoughts about killing Tyrone.

***

"Ma'am, whatever evidence was there, is long gone," the female officer said.

"I know."

Desmond forced me to go to the police and tell them what Tyrone did to me. Strangely, I think he knew that wouldn't be able to do anything. I think he just wanted to have the assault on record for whatever it was that he was planning to do.

"And you had an affair with him?"

"Yes. But I cut it off, and he just won't leave me alone. And that night, he raped me."

The officer asked a few more questions. She told us we could move forward but that most likely, it would turn into a classic case of he said she said. She did talk me into putting out a restraining order against him. At least that should keep him away from me.

"I'm sorry. I should've stayed that morning."

"Yeah. You should've, but it's all good. He better not ever come fucking near you again," Desmond said as we walked down the steps of the police station.

"Will we ever get through this? This is a lot to come back from and…"

Desmond grabbed my hand. "I'm not going anywhere."

Desmond told me that he was coming back home, just in case Tyrone tried to show up again. He said he would sleep in the now-empty guest bedroom as we continue to go to counseling to work on our marriage. And then, he headed off to work and I headed to lunch with the ladies. It wasn't our scheduled one, but I guess everyone needed a drink or conversation, so we planned a late lunch for that day.

"I'm getting a divorce," Tierra said as soon as she sat down.

"What!" I yelled.

"I thought he was Mr. Perfect," Dejah said smugly.

"Oh, he is. I just don't want to leave. I can't leave. I have the salon. My clients. My daughter loves it here and has her friends and father's family. I just can't leave. And I can't make him stay." Tierra shrugged. "He told me that he was opening the gym even before we got married. I thought I would be ready for the change. I wanted to be ready. But I'm not. And I can't ask him to give up his life's dream for me. So, he's still moving, and we're getting a divorce."

None of us knew what to say. Finally, Nicole broke the silence.

"Well, damn, I already put in my notice that I was moving," she complained. "Oh well, guess it all worked out since I found the perfect family for the baby."

"What do you mean?"

"I went ahead with the plan to put her up for adoption. It's the best thing for everyone involved. I don't ever want to see David again. And I just don't think mentally I can take on being her mother right now. It's what's best for her. And no matter what any of you say, I'm doing it. And no, I don't want any of you to get her because I don't want to have to see her."

Again, there was an awkward silence. No one knew how to respond, and no one knew what to say. So, for a while, we all just sat there and ate, looking at people as they walked by.

"Are things getting better with you and Tyree?" I finally asked.

"They're still the same. He's trying though. I can say that much."

"Good. Well, Desmond is moving back home."

"What! Good!"

"Yeah, and he made me go to the police station this morning about Tyrone. I told them he raped me, but of course, there's no evidence. It was just my word against his. And I took out a restraining order on him."

"Oh, really?" Dejah asked. "Well, I guess he said fuck that restraining order then," she nodded at Tyrone's car passing by. "That fool is crazy! I hope you and Desmond got a gun because from the looks of it, he might need to be put down like the dirty dog that he is."

"I'm hoping it doesn't come to that. I just want him to go away. He has plenty of women. I don't get why he's so hellbent on bothering me."

"You must got some good ass pussy," Tierra laughed. "I'm sorry. I know this isn't a funny situation. But let me borrow it. I'm gonna' need it to find me a new husband. I got lucky with this one."

"Tell the truth, his dick little, ain't it?" Nicole asked Tierra. "He has too many muscles to be holding down there. Come on, you can tell us."

Tierra blushed. "What I look like telling y'all that? Just know it gets the job done."

"Translation...that dick is little!" Dejah laughed, and so did the rest of us.

I stared at them, secretly happy that our circle would remain the same and happy that Tierra and Nicole wouldn't be moving away.

I had a feeling that whatever was up ahead, I was going to need them.

All of them.

***

"No! Stop! No!"

I jumped up in a cold sweat. My bedroom light came on, and Desmond appeared in the doorway.

"That's your third nightmare this week."

"I'm sorry."

"You don't have to apologize."

Desmond sat on the edge of the bed.

"It's always the same dream."

"I don't want to hear it. It's going to make me want to..."

I took a deep breath.

"I'll be fine. You have work in the morning. Go back to bed."

"You sure?"

"Yes."

After staring at me for a few more seconds, Desmond got up and headed back to the guestroom.

I forced myself to lay back down.

In the dream, I'm running from Tyrone. He's chasing me with a knife. And no matter what I do, in the end, he always catches me and kills me.

This is one dream that I'm praying doesn't come true.

I managed to dose off, and a few hours later, I woke up to an empty house. It was a Saturday. I figured Desmond had taken the kids out and about to give me some peace and quiet.

I was almost afraid to be home alone. I always felt like Tyrone was somewhere watching, waiting.

Thoughts of him and what he might do to me were consuming me. I poured myself a drink and decided to take a long, bubble bath.

I turned on some music, and once the tub was full of water, I got inside.

I closed my eyes as I rested my head.

I tried to think happy thoughts. I just wanted to relax and breathe.

My eyes were only closed for a minute or so before I heard a loud noise.

"What was that?"

I tapped my phone to turn off the music on my phone.

I listened.

There it is again.

It wasn't as loud as it was the last time, but there was a noise.

My heart was beating so fast that I could hear it thumping in my ears.

Terrified, soaking wet, I tiptoed out of the bathroom and down the hallway. I looked around, and then I rushed towards the window to look outside. No one was there, and Desmond and the kids weren't back.

After checking the lock on the front door, shivering, I headed towards the kitchen.

I checked the back door and glanced into the backyard. I listened.

I waited to hear the sound again.

Thud.

There it is!

What is that?

I rushed back into the living room, and then I just stood there. And then out of nowhere, I heard pounding, as though it was coming from a window, down the hallway, and I lost it. I completely freaked out, opened the front door, and ran out of the house butt naked.

Looking behind me, I hurried down the steps.

"Bailey! Bailey!"

I didn't even notice that Desmond and the kids had arrived.

Immediately, Desmond grabbed me and wrapped his arms around my naked body.

"What's wrong? What's wrong?"

"I was in the tub....and...and..." I tried to catch my breath. "I heard something. I don't know but I heard."

"Kids, get back in the car," Desmond ordered them. "Get in the car, Bailey."

Desmond hurried inside the house as I got in the car with the kids and locked the doors.

"Mommy, are you okay?"

"Yes, baby. Mommy just heard a noise and got scared."

"Oh, daddy will protect you. He's not scared of anything."

I watched the house, waiting for Desmond to reappear. Finally, he came back outside and walked around the house. Before long, he came back around to the front and went back into the house.

He came out with my robe.

I rolled down the car window.

"I didn't see anything."

"I heard something. I swear I did."

"What did you hear?"

"Like a loud noise. Like someone was banging on the window or something."

Desmond waited for me to unlock the car door, and then he helped me into my robe.

"I didn't see anything. I checked everywhere. I even checked the windows. They were locked. Doesn't seem like anyone has been messing with them."

"Desmond, I swear to you, I heard something. I promise you I did."

Desmond got the kids out of the car.

"It's okay. I believe you. But whatever it was, it's gone now. And I'm home. I'm here. I'll protect you."

"Told you, mommy."

The kids ran ahead, and Desmond held my hand.

I know what I heard.

I know I'm not crazy.

God, please don't let me be going crazy!

***

"You're not supposed to be near me!"

"Fuck that piece of paper! If I want to see you, I'm going to see you. Period."

"Then you're going to jail!"

I pulled out my cell phone. Tyrone slapped it out of my hand.

"You changed your number again. Why are you making things so difficult? Why can't things just go back to how they were between us? We used to get down. I know you miss that shit."

"No, I don't. And I meant just what I said. This is your first and only warning. Come around me again and your ass is going to jail! And I mean it!"

I bent over to pick up my phone. And right there, on a busy sidewalk, Tyrone pushed me down.

"Fuck you then, bitch!"

Tyrone hurried away.

"Bailey! You okay?"

I looked up and saw Michael pulling me up from the ground.

"Hold on."

Michael took off running. I kept my eyes on him and saw him push Tyrone. Tyrone turned around, and Michael punched him right in the face. Tyrone went down. And hit the sidewalk.

Out cold.

I rubbed my knee and fixed my dress as Michael headed towards me.

"I saw that fool push you down. What the fuck is his problem?"

"Michael, you didn't have to do that for me."

"It wasn't just for you. It was for all women."

"I wouldn't want you to get in any trouble because of me."

"I'm good, okay? Besides, my brother is the DA. I'll be fine."

Michael helped me get myself together.

I was starting to think he was my guardian angel or something.

"Are you going to be okay? Do you need me to wait around for you?"

I was headed inside of the library.

"No. I think I'll be okay."

I glanced at Tyrone. He was still lying on the ground with people all around him trying to get him up.

"After that, I doubt he comes bothering me. At least not today. Thank you. Seriously. Thank you."

Michael patted his chest, right near his heart.

With a sore knee, and replaying what had just taken place, I headed inside of the library. A part of me wanted to just get in my car and drive home, but I had some work to do, and I couldn't let Tyrone stop me.

I was doing some research for my new book, and I needed to grab a few books from the shelves.

I found a few that I needed and decided to take a seat at one of the tables and start reading. I've always loved to read. I can remember being a little girl, lying in the field of sunflowers in my grandmother's backyard, reading from sun-up to sun-down. She would bring me snacks and sweet tea and tell me to stay out there reading for as long as I wanted to. There was nothing like it. No better feeling than getting lost in between the pages of a good book. That's why my next book had to be one of the best I've ever written. And with all I've been going through lately, hopefully, some of it made for good novel inspiration.

I heard the chair scrape against the floor as she dragged it from underneath the table.

Staci, my friend Nicole's child's father's wife, sat down in front of me.

"When is your friend due?"

"I don't know. Why don't you go and ask your husband?"

"He said he isn't sure."

"Umph, how sad. You married a dirtbag."

I glanced back at my book.

"Did she really not know that he was married?"

"No. She didn't. Nicole isn't like that. She would've never got into bed with him if she'd known from the beginning. You've seen her. Does she look like she has to settle for a man like David? She's never had a problem getting a man, that's for sure. And she sure as hell wouldn't have chosen a married one."

"I have loved him for so, so long. Cheating on me is one thing. Getting another woman pregnant is something else," Staci said. "It bothers me. It's all I think about. I'm a good woman. A good wife. A good mother to his kids. But this...a baby...I just can't deal with it," Staci stood up. "Tell your friend I wish her the best of luck. And tell her that I wish she'd chosen someone else husband." And with that, she walked away.

There was a sadness in her eyes. A cry for help in her voice.

I told myself to mind my business, but something inside of me told me that she was a woman about to do something crazy, or worse.

"Staci..." I called after her.

She turned around with tears in her eyes.

"I have an idea..."

***

Chapter 6

"What's all this?"

"This is dinner."

Desmond pulled out my chair.

He's been back in the house for over two weeks now, and though things were far from perfect, every day, things started to feel more and more normal.

"Wow, this looks really good."

Desmond had flowers and candles all over the place. And he'd cooked a whole chicken, loaded mashed potatoes, string green beans and rolls.

"I do what I can, you know," he smiled as he took a seat across from me.

He poured us both a glass of wine, and then he held up his glass.

"A toast...to new beginnings."

"To new beginnings," I agreed.

After taking a sip of wine, Desmond prepared my plate.

"So, remember that promotion I told you about?"

"Yes."

"Well, I got the job...if I want it."

"You're talking about the job that requires you to move?"

Desmond nodded.

"Do you want it?"

He shrugged. "I don't know. It's a hell of an opportunity. Moving would be a fresh start. A new beginning...for us."

"Us?"

"Yeah. I mean, after all that has happened, wouldn't you agree that a fresh start might just be what we need?"

"I swear it would be. I've even thought about it, to be honest. But there's just one problem. I have a company... here."

"I know."

"I can't leave," I said to Desmond. "Even if a little part of me wants to, I can't leave. I can't relocate. Not yet."

He stared at me for a while, as though he was reading my body language. "I know," is all he said. "It just would've been a hell of an opportunity."

I exhaled. "I don't want to keep you from something you want to do."

"You're not keeping me from anything. It's fine."

For the most part, we ate in silence. We said a few words here and there, but there was so much tension in the room that a knife couldn't cut it.

"I want us," I said finally.

"I do, too," Desmond agreed.

I could tell that he was still thinking about the job opportunity, so I kissed him in hopes of easing his mind.

"I want new beginnings, new memories, new moments, new---everything with you."

"I'll choose you over that job any day. You know that, right? I'll choose you every single time," Desmond said.

I knew he meant his words.

I kissed him again, and I pulled him in close to me. Desmond's kisses were strong, passionate, and once he started to bite on my bottom lip, I knew that he was about to put some loving on me that I would never forget.

This is the version of him that I'd been missing. Had he made me feel like I feel right now, I would've never cheated on him.

Desmond picked me up and sat me on the edge of the kitchen table. He pushed the food out of the way before laying me on my back.

"This is what I've been waiting to eat all night long," he mumbled, staring my pussy in the face.

And without hesitating, he placed his mouth on me, and just as he started to suck, and I started to coo...

"What the fuck!"

A flaming bottle came through the living room window. Desmond rushed over to it, picked it up, and instinctively tossed it back outside.

He patted a small flame on the curtains, before running outside.

My heart was beating faster and faster. I was starting to panic because I couldn't seem to slow it down. Finally, Desmond came back inside.

"Are you okay?"

I nodded.

"I didn't see anyone outside." Desmond walked towards the window. "If we hadn't been here, the whole house would've been burned down. What if the kids were here? What if…"

We both just looked at each other. Neither of us had to say what we already knew.

"Tyrone did this," Desmond growled.

"I know," I admitted. "What in the hell are we going to do?"

***

"What is she doing here?" Nicole asked me.

"Well, I thought it would be a good idea for the two of you to talk, without David here."

"What are we going to talk about? What do you want us to do swap lies?"

"No. But I'm sure both of you have real questions. Her husband is having a baby on her. I know you're not married, but that hurts. You know how much I hurt Desmond with my situation that's going on. And you're completely innocent in all of this. And so is the baby. I just thought it would be good for the two of you to have a big girl conversation. That's all. I'll be over here working if you need me."

I walked away from the table.

I called to check in with Desmond to see how the security installation at the house was going on, and then I checked my emails to see if our lawyer had emailed us back. If Tyrone came anywhere near me or my family again, he was going to regret it.

We had the flaming bottle checked for fingerprints.

Of course, there weren't any on them. The police suggested that we up our security. So, we were getting cameras put in around the house and motion detectors.

I glanced over at Nicole and Staci. They were talking. I had a feeling this was going to be good for both of them. Who knows, this may help Nicole decide to keep her baby.

"Hey, girl, what's up?" I answered my phone for Dejah.

"Well, can I come back to your house again? I think Tyree and I are done, for real this time. And on top of that, I think I'm pregnant."

"Are you serious?"

"Yes. I'm pretty sure that I am. This couldn't be happening at a worse time."

For a while, I listened to Dejah vent. I also told her about what had been going on in my life and let her know that I was unsure of how safe she and the kids would be at my house. We barely wanted to keep our kids there these days. Nevertheless, I told her it was okay for her and the kids to come over. I guess that just means that Desmond had to officially move back into our bedroom.

Good.

I found myself constantly apologizing for everything that was going on. Who knew that Tyrone would turn out to be so crazy? It was starting to piss me off because I was already trying to rebuild my marriage, and he seemed to be making it harder and harder for us to forget about him and move forward.

It was hard to forget my infidelity if the person keeps showing up or keeps becoming a topic of conversation.

The sudden shouting caused me to look in the direction of the women.

"I hope you and your baby die! Do you hear me? I hope both of you just die!" Staci yelled at Nicole and stormed out of the café. I headed for Nicole.

"What happened? Why did she say that? What did you say to her?"

"The truth."

I could see the frustration all over Nicole's face.

"I didn't know David was married in the beginning. But even when I found out, I didn't leave him alone. I still had some crazy hope that we would be a family. I know that makes me a bad person, and maybe it's just the hormones, but I did feel that way for a moment. Now, him, her, and the kids can die for all I care. I know you were trying to help, but I don't need it." Nicole stood up. "I'm getting rid of this baby, and I want to forget that David ever existed. Okay? That's all I want. I don't have too many more weeks to go. I just want it all to be over."

Nicole hugged me and kissed my cheek.

"I'm sorry. I was just trying to help."

"I know." She said. And then she wobbled out of the café.

Shortly after, I gathered my things and headed out of the café too.

"If I didn't know any better, I would say you were stalking me," I said to Michael, literally bumping into him as soon as I was out of the building.

"I was just about to say the same thing. I come here to write all the time."

"Really? Today was my first day coming here. It does have a nice vibe, though."

"And I love the food."

"Maybe we can get together and write here sometime soon."

"It's a deal."

Michael smiled at me, and then he walked inside the café. I hadn't been to the office in three days, so I headed that way. I only planned to stay for a few hours since the kids were coming back home today.

The rest of the day was quiet.

I got a ton of work done, and I managed to start a new chapter in my own book in between reviewing submissions.

"Oh, my God!" I heard my assistant say.

I rushed out of the office to see what was going on. She was looking at the tv, hanging on the wall in the waiting area. I turned it up.

The café that I'd just left a few hours ago was in the background. I listened to the news reporter as she said a man was gunned down coming out of the café.

And then the next thing I saw was his picture.

Michael's.

The reporter said that witnesses didn't see who killed him. Someone in a mask walked up to him, shot him and then ran away.

I sat down.

I couldn't breathe.

Michael is dead.

And...and...I think it's all my fault.

***

"I thought you said he was married," Desmond asked me as we headed out of the church.

"What?"

"You told me that Michael was married. He was divorced, but not married."

"Well, he told me he was married. And do we really have to talk about this right now?"

It was wrong to lie on a dead man, but I didn't want to argue with Desmond. I was already torn up inside knowing that it was my fault that Michael was dead in the first place.

There's no doubt in my mind about who killed Michael.

Tyrone did it.

I couldn't prove it, but I knew he did it.

I tried to tell the police that, but without proof and evidence, there was nothing that they could do.

"I wonder if they'll find his killer," Desmond said.

I decided that it was best not to tell him that Michael had come to my defense and knocked out Tyrone.

"I hope they do. He was a really nice guy."

Desmond and I drove in silence all the way home.

We now had cameras around the house, so we were just waiting for Tyrone to try something else crazy so that we could have him locked away.

"I'm just going to sit out here for a while, if that's okay."

"Sure," Desmond kissed my cheek and left me on the front porch.

The guilt of what happened to Michael was eating me up inside. I knew something bad was going to happen when he kept coming to my rescue. I didn't think that he was going to end up dead, but I knew that Tyrone was going to do something. And there was nothing that I could do to stop it.

Now that everything was happening, and the more I thought about it, I realized that Tyrone showed me who he was in the very beginning.

I could remember how possessive he seemed, but I thought it was just because he wanted me as bad as I wanted him. I can remember hearing him on the phone making threats to people, but I figured it was all talk and that he didn't mean them. I can remember him thinking I was asleep after sex, and him saying that I belonged to him inside my ear.

He meant everything he said in that crazy, twisted mind of his. And now I was more afraid than ever.

If he killed Michael…does that mean he'll try to kill Desmond to?

Is it safer to get away from Desmond to keep him and my family safe?

"Hey," Dejah walked outside onto the front porch. "Desmond told me you were out here. Sorry, I couldn't go to the funeral with you. This morning sickness is whooping my ass already."

Dejah was, in fact, pregnant, but she hasn't told Tyree yet, and she still wants a divorce.

"Dej…Tyrone killed Michael."

"What!" She screamed.

I hung my head and started to fill her in. I told her about the night in the bar that Michael came to my defense, and then I told her about the day he knocked Tyrone out. "He knocked him out because he pushed me down. I knew something bad was going to happen. I'm telling you it was Tyrone who killed him. Whether he did it himself or got someone else to do it. And it's all my fault. I feel horrible. Michael is dead because of me."

"You don't know that. Maybe it wasn't Tyrone."

"Trust me. It was." I shook my head. "Like, what am I supposed to do at this point? Give him what he wants so that he doesn't hurt anyone else around me?"

"Girl, that pussy must really be good. I mean, is it dipped in gold or something? Can I at least smell it?"

"Dejah! I'm serious!"

"Hell, I'm serious too! If Tyrone did kill Michael for whatever he did to defend you, he's about ten steps past being pussy whipped. I don't know what you're going to do."

There is nothing that I can do at this point.

There's no way to bring Michael back from the dead. And there's no way in hell that I'm ever sleeping with Tyrone again.

"I feel like a sitting duck."

"Girl, this will make one hell of a book. The perfect storyline," Dejah shrugged. "Maybe that's why all of this is happening. Your other books didn't have this much juice. And baby, this here is some psycho juice that will definitely make good reading material. Your life has literally become a best-selling novel."

"There has to be something I can do."

"Wait. If Tyrone is still on his crazy bullshit, it won't be too much longer before he does something else. And eventually, he will do something stupid. Just wait. And be ready."

That's all I can do, I suppose.

"I just hope he doesn't hurt anyone that I love. Desmond. The kids. You and the kids."

"Oh, I brought my gun with me. I'm going to light his ass up like a Christmas tree if he comes over here bothering me. He better shoot me before I shoot him, or his ass is dead."

Tyrone.

Dead.

That would be a dream come true right about now.

***

"There's something that she's not telling me," Desmond told our therapist.

"Bailey, are you keeping things from your husband."

"Nothing that has to do with him."

"Bailey, it doesn't matter if it has to do with him or not. Your trust has been broken. Keeping secrets will slow down the healing process."

I looked at Desmond. "I think Tyrone killed Michael."

Hurriedly, Desmond sat up straight on the couch. "What? Why?"

"One night at the bar, the same night Tyrone raped me..."

"Raped?" Our counselor, Joann, spoke up. Hurriedly, I filled her in since I'd told Desmond that I wasn't ready to tell her that part a while ago. So, we'd been leaving it out of the sessions on purpose.

"Anyway," I said, facing Desmond again. "He told Tyrone to leave me alone that night. And then not too long ago, one day, Tyrone pushed me down."

"He did what?" Desmond yelled and stood up.

"Sit down, please," I pulled at his jeans. Desmond was angry, but he sat down per my request. "Tyrone pushed me down, and just so happens, Michael was there. He saw him and came to my defense. He knocked Tyrone out cold. Right there in front of everyone on the street."

"Why didn't you tell me this, Bailey?"

"I didn't want you to be worried. I didn't want you to be upset. I didn't want you to get mad at me all over again for bringing Tyrone into our marriage in the first place. And I surely didn't think Tyrone would kill Michael because of it."

"So, you really think he's responsible for killing Michael?"

"Yes."

"And you and Michael…did the two of you…"

"No. I swear. But maybe Tyrone thought we did. Maybe he thought Michael had taken his place. Maybe he was jealous. Or maybe he was just embarrassed by the whole knock out thing. I don't know. But I know I'm right. I know he did it. And now I'm worried. I'm scared. I'm scared that Tyrone just might be crazy enough to hurt you, me, the kids…"

"I won't let him do a goddamn thing to my kids! Or us," Desmond growled. "If I have to kill him myself…"

"No! Don't say that."

"She's right," the counselor chimed in. "Let's just calm down. There has to be something else that can be done about this Tyrone character. Discussing killing him isn't one of them."

We finished our session, but I knew the conversation wasn't over. As soon as we were outside, Desmond started up again.

"Where does Tyrone live?"

"Why? You're not going over there."

"Don't tell me what to do," Desmond opened the passenger side door for me. Once I got in, he slammed the door shut.

"Look, he's dangerous. Obviously. I don't want you to get hurt."

"So, what am I supposed to do?" Desmond fastened his seatbelt. "Wait around for him to hurt someone I love? Nah. Fuck that. It's time that we have a conversation. Man to man. And if something pops off, then so be it. But I'm not going to sit around while he does whatever the fuck he wants to do to my family."

"It's me that he wants. Trust me, he will try to come around me again, and when he does, it'll violate the restraining order. I just don't want you to do something stupid. Let the law handle Tyrone. Okay?"

Desmond didn't respond.

I continued to talk to him. I could only hope that he was actually listening to me.

"I pray that the next time you're feeling lonely, unsatisfied, or whatever that you make better choices! Run a goddamn background check or something!" Desmond interrupted me.

"Wow," I exhaled. "So, you do blame me?"

"Of course, I do! Who else am I supposed to blame for all this shit, Bailey? Who else?"

"Blame the psychopath!"

"The psychopath that YOU brought into our lives! The psychopath that YOU fucked! The psychopath that won't leave YOU alone! Of course, this is partly your fault!"

Desmond was speeding.

"Look, you're right, okay? You're right."

Desmond failed to hit the brakes going around the sharp curve.

"Desmond, slow down!"

He didn't respond.

"Desmond! I said slow down!" I yelled.

Desmond suddenly hit the brakes, causing my neck to snap forward and the car behind us to swerve and beep the horn.

"What the fuck are you doing, huh? Are you trying to kill us!"

"I'm sorry," he mumbled. "Are you okay? I'm sorry." Desmond exhaled loudly. "I just want things to go back to how they used to be. Before all of this. Before you decided I wasn't enough. I just want it all back. Is that too much to fucking ask?"

Desmond didn't give me a chance to respond.

He started to drive again and turned the radio up as loud as it could go.

I didn't bother trying to force a conversation. Holding the back of my neck, I stared out the window, knowing that I had to find a way to fix the situation before I lose my husband all over again.

And I'll be damned if I let that happen.

***

"Secretly, I was hoping that he would stay. I was hoping that he would choose me, you know?" Tierra frowned. "I told him not to give up his dreams, but I was hoping that he wanted me and our marriage more. He didn't. I signed the divorce papers this morning," she concluded, taking a sip of her mojito.

"Awww, I'm sorry, Tierra." Dejah rubbed her shoulders. "And hell, look at it this way, you are not alone. Tyree and I are getting a divorce too."

"What? Really?"

"Really. We should've never got married. Everything was so much better, easier before we exchanged vows."

"What is he saying about the baby?" I asked her.

"What is there to say? I finally told him. The baby is coming, regardless, but I'm sure that I don't want to be married anymore. I want to be free. I want to feel life again. Marriage just feels so heavy. Or maybe it's just that being married to him feels heavy. I don't know if that means we'll never be together again, but I want a divorce," Dejah shrugged. "It's what's best."

Divorce isn't what's best for me.

Divorce isn't even an option as far as I am concerned.

Desmond has been giving me the silent treatment for the past three days. He hasn't said one word to me. And since yesterday, I stopped trying to push him to have a conversation. I know what the problem is. I just don't know how to fix it.

"I hope you don't rush to get married next time around," Nicole said to Tierra.

"I hope you don't get pregnant by a married man next time around," Tierra shot back at her with a smile. "Too soon?" she asked, noticing Nicole's face.

"Bitch," Nicole growled, but she managed to chuckle.

"I miss the conversations where we were all happy and all in a good space."

"Me too."

"Me three."

"Me fooooouuurrr! Owww!" Nicole touched her belly.

"What? What is it? Is something wrong?"

She frowned. "I don't know if that was a kick or something else, but it hurt like hell."

"You still have over a month left, right?"

Nicole nodded. "Owwww! There it goes again!"

"Maybe it's Braxton Hicks."

"It's my stomach. And my chest." Nicole stood up. "Something is wrong."

"Nicole, baby, you're bleeding. We have to get you to the hospital!"

All at once, we all started to panic. We ran around like chickens with our heads cut off trying pay our tab, gather our things, and get Nicole to the hospital.

Once we got Nicole inside Tierra's car, with Dejah in backseat helping her, I told them I would meet them there.

"Hey, baby," I heard just as I opened the car door.

Instinctively, I pressed Desmond's number on my cell phone.

"Tyrone, you're not supposed to be around me," I got inside my car, and as I attempted to shut my car door, Tyrone grabbed it.

"Just give me that pussy one more time, and I'll leave you alone. I promise."

He smiled as though he still thought I found him attractive.

"Let go of my car door! Stop following me! And stay away from me! Oh, and don't think I don't know what you did. To Michael…"

"Excuse me, I have no idea what you're talking about," Tyrone said sarcastically. But the smirk on his face told me he did. He did it. We both know he did it. But I'll never be able to prove it.

"Please, let go of my door."

"One more time in the car. For old times' sake," Tyrone inched toward me.

"No! I'm calling the police."

"No. What you're going to do is…"

Suddenly, I started to press down on my horn, and I didn't let off of it. People started to notice and head our way. Finally, Tyrone laughed and started to walk away.

"Ma'am, are you okay?" A woman asked.

I stopped pressing the horn.

"Yes. That man is not supposed to be around me. I thought he was going to hurt me."

I glanced at my cell phone.

I could hear Desmond screaming my name.

"Can I take your name and number, just in case I need a witness to testify that he was around me?"

The lady gave me her information, and finally, I was able to put my seat belt on and put the phone to my ear.

"Bailey, are you okay? Did he hurt you?"

"No. But he violated the restraining order. His ass is going to jail."

"What did he say? What did he do?"

"You couldn't hear him?"

"Barely."

Desmond and I talked about Tyrone all the way to the hospital.

"Hey guys, I'm sorry. That fool Tyrone…"

I noticed Tierra and Dejah's face.

"What? What's wrong? Is Nicole okay? Did she have the baby?"

"The baby is going to be fine."

"And Nicole?"

Tierra started to whimper. "They say she lost a lot of blood. They were able to go in and get the baby out, but they're not sure…"

"Not sure of what?"

I pushed passed them to look inside the room.

The doctors were working on Nicole. She had a tube down her throat, and honestly, she looked…dead.

"They're not sure if she's going to wake back up."

Dejah explained that they discovered some kind of blood clot and that Nicole started to hemorrhage during delivery.

"She didn't even want the baby. And now…now she might die because of it." Tierra said through her tears.

"Guys, Nicole is strong. She's going to make it through this. For now, we just have to be strong for her. And we have to be here for her when she wakes up. She will wake up. I promise you, she will. Where is her baby?"

"They took her to clean her up. She's almost a month early and still almost eight pounds."

"Goddamn! I knew she was going to be big."

"And she looks just like Nicole, too."

"They asked us if we knew who the father was," Dejah mentioned. "We told them no. We told them that we would take care of the baby."

"You know Nicole had a family that she planned to let adopt her."

"We know. But if we lose Nicole…"

"We won't lose her," I said. "We won't."

For hours, we sat there, waiting for something to change. Waiting for Nicole to wake up, or for the doctor to say that she was going to make it, for sure, but that news never came. We were all able to see and hold the baby. She's so beautiful and precious that I knew once Nicole saw her, she was going to fall in love with her and want to keep her.

We did find out that if we didn't know who the father was, that they would have to notify DCFS for the next steps. Of the three of us, I was the one most stable on paper and would have the best chance of getting temporary custody of her if it came to that.

But I told the ladies that we needed to call David.

It was in the best interest of the baby.

After leaving the hospital, I headed to the police station. Tyrone needed to be the least of my worries for a while, so I marched inside and told them that he violated the restraining order. I gave them the information about the witness, and I told them, the sooner they arrested him, the better.

And finally, after a long horrible day, I headed home.

Desmond was sitting on the front porch waiting for me.

"Where are the kids?"

"All of them are watching a movie."

I noticed that Dejah's car wasn't in the driveway. She might still be at the hospital.

"How are you holding up?"

I sat down beside Desmond on the porch.

"I just want Nicole to be okay."

Desmond wrapped his arms around me.

"And I want us to be okay."

"We will be."

"You really think so?"

"I hope so."

"And what if we're not? What if everything gets worse? What if we can't get back what we once had?"

"Let's not think like that, okay?"

I nodded. "Oh, look at the baby."

I showed him pictures of Nicole's baby on my cellphone. I also told him about the temporary custody if it came down to it. He and I both knew that we didn't need anything else on our plate right now, but there was no way in hell that I would let that baby get lost in the system if David didn't want to step up.

Desmond understood.

"Will you hold me tonight? Just hold me like you used to. I just need…"

"You don't have to say anything else," Desmond interrupted me, stood up, and reached for my hand.

I love this black man.

Correction…I love my black man.

And I'll never do anything to jeopardize our marriage again.

***

"I'm afraid for my life. I'm afraid for my family's life. All I wanted was for him to stay away from me. That's it," I said to the judge.

Tyrone didn't so much as look in my direction.

His lawyer spoke next.

She was definitely no public defender. I could tell by the way she spoke and the way she carried herself, that she was well paid, and she was nothing to play with.

I wondered how Tyrone could afford her. If I had to guess, he was probably screwing her brains out.

We left the courtroom, unsure of what the outcome was going to be. For now, Tyrone was still in jail, and for now, that would have to do.

"Date night, don't be late," Desmond said as we headed in different directions.

"I won't be."

With Tyrone in jail, I was finally sleeping at night. I didn't feel so heavy. I wasn't looking over my shoulder every second of every day. And Desmond and I were getting along.

I drove to work, talking to Dejah was at the hospital with Nicole.

Five days after giving birth, and things still weren't looking good.

"She looks so peaceful. As though she wants to stay wherever she is. As though she doesn't want to come back to this crazy world."

"Well, she has to come back. We're waiting on her. And her daughter is waiting on her too." I opened my mouth to say something else, but someone caught my eye. "Dejah, guess who's standing in front of my building."

"Who?"

"Staci. David's wife."

"How the hell does she know where you work?"

"I'm sure I mentioned it to her. Anyway, I'll call you back."

I got out of my car and approached her.

"I heard about your friend. David told me."

"Has he been to the hospital?"

"No. And he doesn't plan to go up there. He wants to save our marriage."

"What does that have to do with the baby?"

"Everything," she shrugged. "I didn't sign up to raise my husband's mistress' baby."

I exhaled. As a wife, I tried to understand. But as a friend...

"Look, I know that what happened between your husband and Nicole was hurtful, but the baby is innocent. She deserves to be with at least one of her parents. And why did David send you here? I called him."

Staci exhaled and pulled out papers from her purse.

"He said it was my choice. And...I'm choosing my marriage. Without the baby," she handed me the papers.

"This is David signing over all rights to the baby, to you, if you want them. If not, I pray that a loving couple adopts her and loves her far more than David and I ever could. I just can't look at her every day, knowing how she got her. I wish I was that strong. I'm not."

And with that, Staci walked away.

I wish I could hit her with my car and get away with it, but a part of me understood. And now, I understood how much my infidelity hurt Desmond more than ever.

And tonight, I was going to show him just how sorry I truly am.

"And why are you frowning this morning?" I asked Sage.

She hesitated. "I think I've been ghosted. I fooled around with this guy, and he hasn't called me back in days."

I chuckled. "Let me tell you something. You're young. You're sexy. There's going to be ten other guys. Don't worry about him. It's his loss. Not yours."

I headed inside my office and closed the door behind me.

Today was the day I looked over Michael's book. I was still going to publish it, and all royalties were going to go to his ex-wife and son.

I still wish there was some way that I could prove that Tyrone killed him. With a murder charge, I would never have to worry about Tyrone again.

Nevertheless, I was going to enjoy this peace while it lasted.

"So, you changed the plans?"

Desmond smiled at me, meeting me outside of the hotel later that evening.

"Your wife asked me to come down here and get you."

I was dressed in a sexy maid outfit, and I was attempting to disguise my voice.

Desmond looked at me confused.

"Just play along."

Desmond followed me inside the hotel.

"Your wife told me that she hopes that you're ready for all that's in store for you tonight."

"Where is my wife exactly?"

"She will join us later. For now, I'm in charge."

I was trying not to giggle.

I could tell that Desmond was excited.

I wanted him to feel special.

Tonight is the night that my husband falls madly in love with me again.

We walked inside our hotel suite, and I smiled at the expression on Desmond's face.

"Wow! You really outdid yourself."

Candles and flowers were all over the place, and a spread of food was on a table near the balcony.

"Sit. I'm here to cater to you. Is that okay?"

"Hell yeah," Desmond chuckled.

I helped him get comfortable, and then I fixed him a plate.

I sat next to him, and slowly, I started to feed him.

"You don't have to lift a finger right now. I'm going to take good care of you."

"Well, can I take you home? My wife can stay wherever she is." Desmond laughed. "I can get used to this."

I opened his beer and held up the bottle for him to take a sip.

"Your wife tells me that you're such an amazing husband. She says with you, she feels safe and secure. She says that no one has ever loved her as much as you do."

"Now, she might be right about that."

Desmond allowed me to feed him a spoon full of rice I'd ordered.

"She wanted me to tell you that you are the love of her life. She says that she will spend the rest of her life making things up to you. And she also wanted me to tell you that she was going to fuck the shit out of you tonight."

"Is that right?"

I nodded.

We smiled at each other as I fed him for a little while longer. Finally, I stood up.

"Well, it was nice meeting you. My time is up. Your wife will be in shortly."

Desmond chuckled as I rushed to the bathroom.

Hurriedly, I changed out of my sexy maid outfit into a nice black, see-through lingerie set. I slipped on the black tights, and six-inch leather heels to match, and then I did my make-up in dark eyeshadow, tons of mascara, and red lipstick just like Desmond likes it.

It's showtime!

"Hey, baby," I said, walking out of the bathroom.

Desmond stopped eating and looked at me.

"Damn!" He grinned.

"I guess that means you like what you see?"

"I love it."

I smiled at him.

"Pick up your chicken leg," I said to him.

Desmond did as he was told.

"Now, slide back from the table."

Desmond pushed his chair back. Slowly, I got down on my knees in front of him.

"Eat your chicken. Don't worry about what I'm doing," I said, undoing his button and zipper.

I pulled out his dick. He was already hard, which made me all the more eager to please him.

"Whatever I do, don't stop eating your chicken," I instructed him. Desmond took a bite of his chicken and nodded his head.

And for the next few minutes, I sucked his dick, and Desmond moaned in between eating his chicken.

I sucked and sucked until his cum inflated my jaws.

I swallowed it.

"Now, we can finish eating."

Desmond stared at me in pure lust as I sat across from him.

"Eat. You're going to need your energy."

And I meant just that.

By the end of the night, Desmond and I fucked on the balcony, the shower, back to the balcony again, on the table of food, and finally, we made it to the floor.

"Oh my God," was all Desmond could say as we laid on the floor breathless. "That was amazing. Everything was amazing," he said.

"I'm glad you liked it. I owed you this night. I owe you so much more. I love you."

"You don't owe me anything," Desmond said. "And I love you more. I really, really do."

Desmond pulled me closer to him, and I laid my head on his chest. I listened to the sound of his heartbeat until his snores filled the room.

I got my husband back.

Tyrone is going to jail, and hopefully, when he gets out, he will have learned his lesson and leave me alone.

I got my life back.

I eased out of Desmond's arms, and feeling inspired, I grabbed my laptop and headed to the balcony to work on my new book.

This was going to be my best book yet.

I can feel it.

***

Chapter 7

"Please, Ms. Birch. Just a few more days," I pleaded with Nicole's mother.

For two weeks, Nicole had been in a coma and was still showing no signs of improvement. They had called in her mother, all the way from Tallahassee, and she seemed anxious to pull the plug on her daughter.

Nicole and her mom never really got along, from what Nicole told us, and I hated the thought of Nicole's life being left in her hands.

Nicole always said that she was money hungry and selfish. She even told us how her mother mistreated her when she was younger because she pretty and had a nice body.

Her mother used to make her wear rags to school while her other siblings got to dress nice. She would call Nicole ugly and say that grown men were going to rape her if they saw her curves. Nicole didn't realize that her mother was actually jealous of her until she was in high school. She said that's when things got worse between them. Nicole said she and her mother got in plenty of fistfights, but that her mother wouldn't put her out because the money she received from her father would stop coming if Nicole didn't live there.

On prom night, Nicole came home to find her gown cut into pieces and her mother holding the scissors. But that didn't stop her. She she was dealing with this older guy at the time who took her out and got her an even better dress than the one her mother destroyed.

Nevertheless, once Nicole graduated high school, she left Tallahassee, and never went back.

Literally.
She never went home for holidays, birthdays, never.

She did say she would call her family once or twice a year, but that was about it. She didn't even want to be bothered with her siblings because they knew she was being mistreated by their mother, and they never said anything. They just looked on, thankful that it wasn't happening to them.

The only good news about Nicole's mother being here is being the maternal grandmother, and because David had signed over all rights to the baby, she was able to stop child welfare services from stepping in. She didn't want to raise the baby herself, but she was giving all rights to me just in case Nicole didn't pull through.

"I have to be back to work in three days. If she isn't up or showing improvement by then..."

"Okay."

Nicole's mother walked out of the hospital room.

"Come on, baby," I held Nicole's hand. "Wake up. Your daughter needs you. We all need you. Wake your ass up! Your evil ass mama is here, and you can't give her the satisfaction of dying. She would enjoy it too much. You can't let her win. Come on. Just wake up."

I sat there for a while longer, trying some natural remedies and methods that I'd found online. I tried a little prayer too. And then finally, after kissing Nicole's forehead, I headed home.

It was my turn to get the baby.

Dejah was still staying at my house, and together, we were handling the baby. We even gave her a name.

Olivia Nicole.

Nicole is going to hate that name if...well, when she wakes up. But she was going to absolutely adore her precious little girl. Hopefully.

As soon as I walked out of the hospital, my phone started to ring.

"Hello, handsome."

"Tyrone is out of jail."

"What! How?"

Desmond went on to explain how Tyrone's badass lawyer was able to get him out of jail on some kind of technicality.

"That's bullshit! Unbelievable!"

"Well, the good thing is the lawyer said if he so much as speaks your name, he's going back to jail for a minimum of two years. He said that we shouldn't have any problems with him ever coming near you again. I want to get you a gun, just in case. We can't play around with someone like him."

A gun?

Desmond has a gun, but I never thought I would need one. But with Tyrone out, and I'm sure he's upset with me, I had a strange feeling that I was going to need it. And I'm going to use it if I have to!

"Shut the hell up, Tyree!" Dejah screamed into the phone just as I walked inside the house.

The baby was crying in her arms. I took her from her.

"Hey, baby, what's wrong, huh?" I spoke to Nicole's daughter as Dejah continued to argue with Tyree.

After fixing the baby a bottle, I stared at her as I fed her. She's so precious. I just can't believe that Nicole was going to give her up, though I understood her reasoning. And I also can't believe that David didn't want to be a part of her life. I vowed right then and there that if Nicole didn't make it, I would do everything in my power to make sure that she has everything that she deserves.

"Ugh, he makes me sick!"

Dejah joined me on the couch. I stared at her stomach. She hadn't started to show yet, but I couldn't wait to find out what she was having.

"Now he's saying that he's not signing the divorce papers."

"Why?"

"He says that he loves me and that he isn't giving up on us." Dejah shook her head. "He found a new job, but that's still not enough. Once we got married, everything changed, and I just don't want to keep going around in circles with him. I want out. I just want out."

"Well, I'm sure he'll sign the papers, eventually."

"He better. Or I'm going to kill him."

"Girl, hush. Hell, worst-case scenario, people move on and date other people and never get a divorce."

"I don't want to be one of those people. He already got me pregnant. That should be enough."

Dejah kissed the feeding baby.

"I hope I'm having a girl."

"Me too!"

"I didn't think I would be excited about it. But with everything going on, it seems like something good in all the mess. I just pray that Nicole pulls through and that everything around us just goes back to normal."

"Well, that's my prayer too. They let Tyrone out of jail."

"Why?"

"Your guess is as good as mine. Clearly, he violated the restraining order, but I guess his lawyer is just a little bit better at working the system than ours. The good thing is, if he ever comes around me again, he'll be looking at a minimum of two years in prison. And he's tough. But I know he doesn't want that. Hopefully, that is enough to keep him away from me. He can move on and ruin some other woman's life. I've had enough."

"I bet your ass won't cheat on your husband again, will you?"

"Girl, never, ever. Like I don't even want other men to look my way at this point."

Dejah chuckled. "I'm glad you and Desmond are working it out. I've always thought the two of you were a good couple and one hell of a team. The two of you give us all hope." Dejah said just as her phone started to ring. "What the fuck do you want, Tyree!?"

She yelled as she headed out of the living room. I couldn't help but smile.

She admired Desmond and my relationship, but for years, I admired hers with Tyree.

Dejah and I have been friends for eight years. When I first met her, she was with her boy's father and unhappy. He was an asshole, and he treated her like a child. Finally, Dejah got the courage to leave him. He told her that she would never find anyone else to love her or put up with her as long as he did.

Two years later, she met Tyree. Tyree and Dejah are complete opposites, but they complimented each other so well. I remember noticing how he would look at her. He would stare at her as though she was the most beautiful woman he's ever seen. He complimented her all the time. He was so good to her kids. He was always surprising her and trying to do things just to make her smile. I would get jealous at times as she told me stories about things he would do for her just because he lovedAherthen he asked Dejah to marry him.

He planned this big party and pulled out every trick in the bag to make his proposal special.

And unfortunately, in front of everyone, Dejah said no.

She told him that she loved him and that she didn't want to be with anyone else other than him, but that she wasn't ready to get married. I think she was just getting a good feel of her freedom, and she didn't want it to be taken away.

And though he was super embarrassed, and his family was upset, Tyree accepted the fact that she wasn't ready, and he stayed right by her side. He continued to love her. He continued to support her. He continued to let her be the wild, crazy, fireball that she was. I just loved the way that he loved her. The way that he stuck by her even when she didn't make sense.

And then over a year ago, years after he's asked her the first time, he asked her to marry him again. That time, Dejah said yes. The only request she had was that they don't have a big wedding.

So, they kept it simple.

A small beach wedding, and on that day, Dejah was genuinely happy. I could see it all over her face. And now…now they just can't seem to get on the same page.

Dejah continued to scream at Tyree. And strangely, it was like music to my ears. I liked having Dejah in the house. She had become a part of my new normal.

Normal.

I miss normal.

I want normal.

And I was praying that everything went back to normal very, very soon.

***

"Why do you insist on driving around these curves so fast? Slow down," I begged Desmond.

"Woman, I got this."

We were headed out for date night.

"No, you don't."

Finally, we pulled up at the restaurant.

"Thank God, we made it," I said sarcastically.

"Come on. I'm ready to eat."

Once we were seated, we didn't hesitate to order a few drinks.

"Shit!"

I noticed him at the exact moment that he noticed me.

"We have to leave."

"What? Why?"

I nodded my head. Desmond turned around. He and Tyrone made eye-contact, and as always, Tyrone grinned.

"He was obviously here first. Come on. Let's just go."

I didn't want to be anywhere near him, with or without a restraining order. I didn't want to see his face.

Desmond stood up.

"You know, I got a word or two to…"

"No! I grabbed his arm. Let's just go."

I pulled Desmond out of the restaurant.

"It's funny how he always seems to just show up. He's always wherever you are."

"I was just thinking the same thing," I agreed with Desmond.

"But we're not going to let him ruin date night. So, what do you want to do?"

I could see the frustration all over Desmond's face. The wheels inside his head were turning, so I spoke to him again, softly.

"Let's just do something wild. Something that will make us both smile and something we will never forget." I paused. "Oooh, I have the perfect idea! Name three places."

"What?" Desmond looked at me confused.

"You heard me. Name three places. It can be anywhere. Indoor, outdoor, whatever. Just three places. Types of places like a bank or church. Just a random place."

"Uh, laundry mat, nightclub and movie theater. Why?" I smiled.

"Your wish is my command. Hand me the keys. I'm driving."

I drove towards the closest movie theater.

Desmond assumed we were going to watch a movie, so he started to suggest movies that he'd been wanting to see. I had other plans.

I told Desmond to just pick a movie, and once he had our tickets, as we walked inside the theater, I told him that we wouldn't be seeing a movie at all.

He questioned me, but I simply ignored him and led him towards the ladies' room.

"What? I can't go in there," Desmond yelled as I tried to pull him inside the bathroom.

"Yes, you can. No one is in here."

I tugged at him a little longer, and finally, I got him into the bathroom and inside the bigger stall.

"You're going to fuck me at all three places you named, tonight," I revealed to him. "Would you rather go inside a movie? That might be more exciting."

"Nah, I'm full of excitement right now. Can't you tell?" Desmond glanced down at his dick.

And just like that, for the next ten minutes, I let him have his way with me. I bite my bottom lip as he pounded me from behind. We had to slow it down twice because people came into the bathroom, but as soon as they were gone, we were at it again.

Finally, I walked out of the bathroom first and then gave Desmond the okay to come out behind me.

"Next up, the laundry mat," I smiled.

We drove past three 24-hour laundry mats until finding one that was deserted.

"I'm sure they have cameras," Desmond looked around the ceiling.

"So."

I walked towards the back of the laundry mat.

"You want me to sit on this table?"

Desmond looked around.

"Just bend over. Just in case someone comes in."

I could've cared less. I just wanted to make new, nasty memories with him.

"They only have that camera up there, and it's facing that way. That's if it even works."

Instead of bending over, I hopped onto the table and opened my legs.

"Fuck me, Daddy."

Desmond's fears and concerns immediately vanished.

I howled inside the laundry mat as we had sex again.

"Two down, one to go," I smiled once Desmond came inside of me. "Do you think you have another nut left in you?"

"Hell yeah, let's do it."

Smelling like sweat and ass, we left the laundry mat and drove towards the club.

"We haven't been to a club in years," Desmond pointed out. "Remember the last time?"

"Yes. Do you remember how drunk we got? And how I peed in the car? Man, those were some good times."

"They sure were. Why did we ever stop? Why did we stop having fun?"

"I don't know," I mumbled. "Life. Marriage. Kids."

Desmond looked at me. "Let's vow to never let that happen again. Let's always find the time to just have fun. Just the two of us. If we can promise to do that, I think we'll be just fine."

"I promised," I smiled. "Now, let's go."

With no panties on, I pulled down my dress, and we headed inside of the club. Once inside, instead of immediately looking for a place to have sex, feeling the music, I started to dance. Desmond was right behind me. He started to grind up against me, and then he asked me if I wanted a drink.

Before we knew it, five drinks in and an hour later, we were still on the dance floor, dancing out of rhythm and dancing to songs we've never even heard of.

All hot and sweaty, Desmond started to kiss me, somewhat reminding me of what we'd come to the club to do. So, I grabbed his hand and headed to a seating area in the back of the club. It was dark, other than a few colorful lights, so I sat Desmond down and then sat on top of his lap.

I'm sure that people would think I was just giving him a lap dance, so I pushed his dick inside me.

"I love you!" I screamed over the music.

Desmond grabbed a handful of my hair and started to kiss me, hard, and full of passion. I started to roll my hips, and just as a new song began to play, my body started to heat up. I found myself rolling and riding his dick to the tune of the music. I was in a zone. I felt so alive and so good that I felt as though I was going to explode. I rode his dick faster and faster and faster...

Just as I started to cum, gunshots rang throughout the club, and my heart dropped. Desmond jumped into protection mode, and with his pants halfway pulled up, he grabbed my hand, and we ran towards the back exit.

Once outside, we kept running all the way to the parking lot, and as soon as we were safe inside our car, we looked at each other and started to laugh.

"Oh, my God!"

"Yeah. That shit was wild."

Desmond pulled out of the parking lot as I rolled down the passenger side window.

"It was, but I loved every minute of it."

"Me too," Desmond reached for my hand. "Me too."

We talked and laughed the whole ride home, and we both agreed that tonight was a night that we would always remember.

***

"It feels weird being here without Nicole," Tierra said.

"Yeah. It does. But it may be something we have to get used to," Dejah shrugged.

"Don't say that."

120

"Well, it's true. We're not going to be able to hold on to her like that forever."

We were at lunch together, and though Nicole's mother had left town, she told us she would be back and that she would be pulling the plug on Nicole.

"I just pray something changes in the next few days."

"And I can't believe David's ass!"

David, Nicole's daughter's father, showed up at the hospital the day before. He said he wanted to see Nicole. He didn't so much as ask how the baby was doing. He only said that he felt it was his fault for Nicole being how she was. He said he felt guilty for putting so much pain and stress on her during the entire pregnancy.

"I can't believe he really doesn't want the baby."

"I think in a way he does. I just think he wants his wife more."

"Well, his wife needs to get over herself!" Tierra rolled her eyes. "Speaking of wife…"

"Oh, hell no!" Dejah said. "You're just getting out of a marriage, Tierra!"

"I know. But Luis needs a green card."

"Who the fuck is Luis?"

Tierra described a sexy Latino man that she was thinking about marrying to keep in the states.

"You need help. You know that, right?" Dejah laughed.

"Shoot, I've already had sex with him. I figured I might as well. Who knows, he might end up being a pretty good husband. I've tried every type of black man there is. Maybe it's time to try something new."

"Was it good? The sex?"

"It was amazing!" Tierra squealed. "Some of the best sex I've ever had! It was passionate, and he was so attentive. Like, he wanted to suck and lick everything. It was all about me. I can definitely get used to that."

"Umph. Maybe I'll try me a good ole' Hispanic man when I pop this baby out of me."

"Yeah, right. Tyree ain't letting you go."

"He doesn't have a choice! He can't make me stay married to him."

We all chuckled.

"And what about you? How are things?" Tierra asked me.

"Everything is fine. They really are."

They truly were.

I'm so in love with my husband. Like all I do is think about him. And I can tell that he's feeling the same way. Whenever we're away from each other these days, we're constantly texting, and when we're around each other, we can't seem to keep our hands off one another. I really do love him. And I just can't imagine my life without him.

"Yeah, I heard you and Desmond fucking the other night, too," Dejah rolled her eyes. "Hell, I couldn't tell which one of y'all was moaning the loudest."

"Shut up!" I nudged Dejah. "You didn't hear shit!"

"Oh, yes I did. One of y'all was hitting high notes and all. I was like damn! It made me a little hot and bothered. I almost snuck out to go give Tyree some ass."

Dejah was laughing so hard that tears came out of her eyes. "Next time, I'm going to crack y'all door open and watch."

"You better not!"

"Watch me."

We laughed for a little longer about the topic.

"And Tyrone?" Tierra asked.

"I haven't heard from him. Or seen him since Desmond and I ran into him at a restaurant a while back. Maybe he has moved on."

"Good. Maybe going to jail was what he needed to get it through his head."

"Maybe."

We finished lunch, and the girls left. I decided to stay and write at the café. Though I hadn't planned on it, initially, I was now writing my first mystery book. In a way, everything that I've been through with Tyrone had somewhat encouraged it.

It was full of drama. It did have a crazy lover in the story. Not quite my situation to the tee, but I was definitely using some events that had taken place this past year as inspiration.

I truly think it's going to be the best book I ever wrote. And maybe Tyrone is to thank for that.

And so, for another three hours, I sat there, ordering sweet tea and daiquiris, writing my heart out.

My book was taking all kinds of twists and turns, and I couldn't wait to see where the story would go.

"Hello?"

I answered my phone and listened to the voice on the other end of the phone. And then, with the biggest smile on my face, I grabbed my things and rushed out of the café, heading to the hospital.

"Hey, beautiful," I chimed.

Nicole half-smiled. She touched her throat as though she couldn't speak.

"It's a miracle. We don't know how, or why, her vitals just got better out of nowhere, and then she just woke up." The doctor said. "We're running some tests now, and we'll be checking for more blood clots. But she's awake. And that's a very, very, good thing."

The doctor left the room.

"I'm so happy," I started to cry. "The other girls are on their way."

Nicole touched her belly.

"She's fine. She's so beautiful too. We named her...Olivia Nicole. I know, you're going to hate it, but we thought..."

Nicole started to whimper. It was as though she wanted to cry, but she couldn't. She still couldn't speak, so I just held her hand.

"I knew you were going to wake up. You're strong. You're a fighter. I just want you to know that I love you, and I'll always have your back. Always. You and that baby will always be able to count on me."

I kissed Nicole's forehead, just as Dejah rushed inside the room.

"Well, it's about damn time that you woke your ugly ass up!"

"Dejah, don't make her laugh!"

"I'm sorry," Dejah walked over and kissed Nicole's face. "I missed you, chick. I don't know what I would've done without you."

Before long, Tierra joined us, and we all just sat there with Nicole, talking to her, and showing her pictures and videos of her beautiful baby. She still couldn't talk, so we were unsure of what she planned to do, but we didn't bother her with too many questions. We were just happy that she was still here with us.

Dejah decided to stay overnight with Nicole, so Tierra and I walked out of the hospital together.

"I'm really happy that everything is working out for you. You've been through a lot, and I'm just glad things are getting better."

"Thank you. And never give up on finding the love that you feel you deserve. You're going to find it. You're going to have everything you want one day. I can feel it."

"Thank you. I really hope so."

We hugged and then went our separate ways.

It was late, but I remembered that I needed to stop by my office, so I drove that way in a hurry.

As soon as I pulled up, my heart dropped into the pit of my stomach. Immediately, I spotted Tyrone's car parked in front of my building.

And then, hand and hand, I saw him and my assistant, Sage, walk out together.

My mouth opened wide.

Sage and I talked, but again, she was younger, so there wasn't but so much I told her about my personal life.

She had no idea about my affair with Tyrone.

I watched her kiss him.

I wonder if he's the man that she said ghosted her a while ago. He was in jail at the time. Maybe that's why he didn't call her or return her calls.

Hmmm…

He's up to something.

And then it hit me, maybe that's why he always seemed to know where I was. Sage kept my schedule. She even penciled in my date-nights with Desmond to make sure I remembered. Maybe some kind of way, he was getting access to her computer or her phone and keeping tabs on me.

Tyrone looked towards my car and grinned just before getting into his truck and driving away.

He had no right to be at my place of business! I'm pretty sure that's some type of violation, and I planned to call my lawyer to find out.

Sage noticed my car and headed my way.

"Sorry, I had some work to finish up late today. I know you and Tyrone know each other, but he said nothing ever happened between you too. So, when he approached me at the bar…"

"Stay away from him, Sage!"

She looked confused.

"He's just using you to get to me."

"Excuse me?" She sounded offended.

"That man raped me. And I have a restraining order against him. He's not supposed to be anywhere near me. And he damn sure shouldn't have been here! He's crazy,

Sage. Do you hear me? That man will ruin your life. Trust me, I know. Stay away from him!"

Sage covered her mouth with her hands. "I'm so sorry. I didn't know. I...I...I didn't know."

"I know. But now you do. He ruined my marriage. He's been stalking me. And I'm pretty sure that he killed Michael."

"Please tell me you're joking."

"I wish I was," I looked at her directly in the eyes. "Mark my words, if you don't leave him alone, now, you're going to regret it."

I could only hope that he wouldn't start stalking her once she cut ties with him, but she vowed to never see or speak to him again.

For her sake, she'd better keep her words.

I asked her if he would have had access to her phone or computer. She told me that sometimes he slept over at her house, so maybe he could have accessed either of them then. She said once, she'd given him the code to her computer because he said he needed to look up something.

I'm sure he found my schedule, and that's why he seems to know where I am before I'm even there.

I drove away from my building completely in my feelings. I was worried about Sage. Maybe I was even afraid for her. I wondered if he was going to do her the same way he did me. I wondered if she would be safe.

I would never be able to live with myself if she got hurt by Tyrone because of me.

No one is safe.

And it's all my fault.

***

"You okay?"

"I'm okay."

"Well, today, you get to go home."

Nicole frowned. "I'm scared. I still don't feel like myself. And I still don't know what to do about the baby. I don't know how I feel. I just know that I'm nervous."

"You don't have to decide right now. Take your time. I got her. I'm enjoying her. And so is Desmond. If you still want to go through with the adoption, that's your choice. I wouldn't fight to keep her."

"I just...I just don't know what I feel."

I helped Nicole put on her shoes.

"Dejah is already at your house. We went to the grocery store, and she's going to stay there with you for a few days. Oh, and your mama said she'll be back."

"Oh, hell no she won't! Keep her away from me! You know that she and I don't get along. Tell her I'm fine and that she doesn't have to come. I'm surprised she didn't tell the doctors to kill me."

"Well, she was damn sure on her way too. I see what you mean about her. I always thought you were exaggerating."

"Nope. That lady is evil. And she hates me just as much as I hate her. She's the reason I've never really wanted kids. I was so damaged by her that I didn't think I would be a good mother. And I didn't want my child to end up hating me the same way I hate her."

"Well, you're nothing like her. You're going to be an amazing mother...if that's what you choose to do."

It took us a while, but finally, we made it to Nicole's house. Once they were all comfortable, Desmond called me to get home with the kids so that he could go out with his friends.

"Can we reschedule our therapy session tomorrow?" Desmond asked. "Tomorrow evening, I'm going to go out with some clients."

"Sure. I'll be home all day tomorrow. I'm going to stay here with the kids and work since Dejah is staying at

Nicole's house to help her. So, canceling tomorrow is actually a good idea."

Desmond and I spoke a little longer, and then he was gone.

I spent the rest of the day and evening playing with the kids, cleaning up, and working on my book. I must've fallen asleep while putting the baby asleep, but the sound of the waiting alarm caused my eyes to pop open.

Immediately, the baby started crying, and the other kids ran into the living room to see what was going on. I glanced at my phone. It was after ten, and Desmond had texted over an hour ago saying that he was going to be late.

My cell phone started to ring, and once I realized that it was the security company, I answered.

"Hello, Mrs. Williams, this is Roy from MSDT Homes Security. Is everything okay?"

I rushed over to the alarm to type in the code.

"Uh, I don't know," I finally responded once the alarm was silenced. The baby was still screaming, but I headed to the window to take a look outside.

"Are you able to check the feed from the cameras around the house while I'm on the phone? I don't see anyone."

"I don't see anything or anyone out there now. Wait…"

My heart was beating faster and faster.

"Someone was out there. They're in all black with a face mask…going back three minutes ago, they were out there. The motion detectors must've set off the alarm. From the two cameras that you have set, around the house, it's hard to tell where they ran off to, but they're gone. I don't see anyone out there now. Would you like for me to call the police?"

"Yes!"

Finally, I headed to pick up the baby. She was still crying, and I tried to rock her and call Desmond at the same time. The police made it there before he did.

"Hi, we got a call that someone was lurking around your house."

"Yes. And I know exactly who it was. His name is Tyrone."

"Did you see him?"

"No. But I have a restraining order on him because he's been stalking and harassing me. It had to be him."

Desmond's car sped into the driveway, and he nearly jumped out of it before he placed it into park. He ran in my direction.

"Are you okay? Is everyone okay?"

I nodded.

"We're going to take a look around the house."

The police walked down the steps of the porch, and immediately, Desmond started to ask more questions.

"Did the man from the security company say she saw someone?"

"Yes. He said someone in all black, wearing a face mask, got too close to the house and set off the alarm."

Desmond walked down the porch steps.

"He must've been trying to come up the steps. See, the motion detection is right there."

"I'm just glad I turned everything on when you left. I was going to wait until you got back, but something told me to set it. I'm glad that I did. Had the alarm not sounded, who knows what would've happened."

My mind was racing.

I'm positive it was Tyrone lurking around, and for the life of me, I just can't understand why he wouldn't just leave me alone already.

"Well, we didn't see anything out of place," the officer said. "We saw a few footsteps in the grass on the other side of your car. Looks like whoever it was standing there for a while. Your car doors are locked, and nothing appears missing from inside through the window. Do you really think it was someone you know?"

"I'm positive. I know it's him. I know that it's Tyrone! I have a restraining order on him, and he hasn't cared about it before, so I'm sure he doesn't now."

Desmond rubbed my back.

"Without for sure proof that he was here, there isn't much we can do. We can take his address, if you have that, and go talk to him."

I gave the officers Tyrone's address, and then they were on their way. Desmond checked my car just to make sure nothing was out of place. It wasn't.

After setting the alarm again, together, Desmond and I made sure the kids were okay, and then we headed back to the living room to talk.

"You okay?"

"Yes. Just feeling a little paranoid. Everything has been going so good. I just..."

"It's okay. Maybe it wasn't him."

"It was him. I know it was him."

"You really think he would risk going to prison by coming here?"

"I don't. He killed Michael so, who knows what he will do."

"You don't know that."

"But I do."

I picked up my phone and called Sage on speakerphone.

I asked her if she'd heard from Tyrone. She said she told him she couldn't talk to him anymore after finding out the truth about him and she said he cursed her out like a dog. He also told her that he didn't want her anyway. And that he wanted me. He was just getting close to her to piss me off.

"Still think it wasn't him?"

Desmond shook his head. "Well, now he knows we have an alarm. He won't come back here."

"That's not enough." I reached for Desmond and the baby and stood up. "It's just not enough. Besides, he's crazy, and he doesn't have his head screwed on right, I don't think he gives a damn about the alarm."

"Then, if he comes in here, he will be dealt with," Desmond assured me. "I got you baby. I promise. I'm not going to let anything happen to you or anyone else in this house. I'll die trying to save you. You know that."

"I do. The problem is, you shouldn't have to. This shouldn't be happening to us. If I were you, I wouldn't want anything to do to with me."

"Well, good thing I'm not you then, huh?"

Desmond smiled and kissed me before leaving the room.

I don't know what I would do if he wasn't here right now. And then again, if he wasn't here, maybe Tyrone wouldn't be bothering me in the first place.

Either way, enough is enough. And something has to give. I can't spend the rest of my life living like this.

Something has to be done about Tyrone.

And soon.

***

I picked the sleeping baby up from the car seat and walked over to Nicole.

She took a deep breath and held out her arms.

Immediately, she smiled.

"Oh, my God. She has my nose."

"Yep. And your eyes. And your lips too," Dejah mentioned. "She's going to be so beautiful. Just like her mama."

Slowly, Nicole started to rock the baby.

"Olivia Nicole," she smiled. "I think I like it." Nicole took a deep breath. "I think I love her."

She started to cry, and both Dejah and I rubbed her back.

"This is my baby. My beautiful, sweet baby. I can't believe I wanted to give her away."

"Wait. So does this mean you're going to keep her?"

Nicole nodded. "Yes. I want my baby. I want my baby."

My heart swelled with so much joy that I started to cry too. This was such good news.

"I was pregnant once. I've never told anybody this," Nicole started. "I was only fifteen. And it was by my mama's boyfriend."

Hurriedly, I wiped the tears from my face.

"At first, I found it disgusting that he would watch me. I would catch him looking at me all the time. And so would my mother. I'm sure it made her hate me even more. And then one day, I was sitting outside, and he came and sat beside me. He asked me why my mother treated me that way. He told me it was wrong. He told me it was abuse. Isn't that something to say, knowing he was lusting over a fifteen-year-old girl? Anyway, he asked me why I was staying there with her and being treated that way. I told him I didn't have anywhere else to go. After that conversation, we started to have one on one conversations more often. And then one day, he came over while my mother was at work. He said he'd left something in their bedroom. I was the only one home. My mama had just pissed me off that morning before she left. She had come into my room, using stuff that I'd had to babysit to buy for myself because she wouldn't buy for me, and she had the nerve to say as long as it was in her house, it belonged to her. And so…"

I held my breath.

Dejah was staring at Nicole, wide-eyed, as though she was in shock.

"So, I walked it to my mother's bedroom. He smiled at me, and I grabbed his dick. He asked me what I was doing and even pretended as though he didn't want me, but I knew he did. His perverted stares told me that he did. And so…I had sex with him in my mother's bed. And I liked it too. I liked the way it felt. And I liked the fact that I knew I was doing something that would hurt her if she ever found out."

"Oh, my God!"

"His ass should've gone to jail! You were just a child."

"I wasn't a virgin. I'd been having sex since I was thirteen years old. I was always looking for attention and love and when a boy gave it to me…I gave him me. Blame my mama for my way of thinking. But yes, he was a grown thirty-something-year-old man." Nicole confirmed. "After we fooled around, he broke up with mama. He used me as an excuse, which only made things worse between us once he was gone. He told her he didn't like how she treated me and that he didn't want to be with someone who does their child the way that she did me. She didn't hit on me or anything; she just didn't really like me. I mean, she really, really didn't like me. She was jealous of me. Anyway, I missed my period, and I had to go to his house. Of course, I didn't want a baby, so he took me to get an abortion. I never saw him again after that, and I made sure that I never had to do that again. I got on birth control, and I stayed on it until…"

"Until you met David."

"I didn't even mean to get off of it. We were out of town, that time he took me to Houston, and I missed my appointment. And when I got back, it completely slipped my mind to reschedule. And by the time I remembered, I was already pregnant."

Nicole exhaled.

"Well, that just means that little Miss. Olivia was meant to be here. That's all that means. She has a purpose. And God has a plan. For both of you."

"Yep. And we got your back. No matter what," Dejah assured her.

"I know. And I love you guys so much. I mean, I really, really, love y'all. Y'all love me more than my real siblings ever have. I appreciate everything. I really do. Thank y'all."

"Hey, no thanks needed. That's what friends...sisters are for."

Since we didn't get to have a baby shower, and because Nicole was keeping the baby, I asked her if she was up for a little shopping. She was slowly getting around, but she said she was up for going to a store or two.

So, together, we all piled into Dejah's car, since it was the biggest, and headed out.

"Oooh, look at these!"

"Oh, my God! Those are really cute," Nicole smiled. "She's about to have me spending all my damn money."

"Girl, me too. I'm already over here telling myself that $500 is my budget."

"Umph, well, she ain't getting but $100 out of this auntie," Dejah laughed. "I'm the cheap one. And I'm buying stuff that she won't need for a year. She's going to grow out of all that stuff y'all buying."

We all continued to talk.

"Nicole?"

We all turned around to face him.

David.

He glanced down at the baby in Nicole's arms.

None of us knew what to say.

Nicole sat on the scooter, and both Dejah and I stood there. All of us were just staring at him.

"Can I see her?"

"Oh, now you want to see her? But I thought you didn't want to have anything to do with her?" Dejah said with an attitude.

Nicole didn't move.

The baby started to move around, and David held out his arms.

"If you pick up that baby, we're done!"

We all looked behind David, at his aggravating wife.

"Do you hear me, David? If you touch that baby, our marriage is over."

"You're just a bitter bitch, aren't you?" Dejah said. The right one was here today because Dejah was surely going to let her know exactly what she thought about her. "It's a damn baby. His damn baby! He has already signed over his rights to keep you happy. Damn! Let the man at least hold the baby that he's never going to get to see grow up."

I could tell that David was thinking about his next move. And knowing that his wife was going to be upset, still, he held out his arms.

"Can I hold her?" he asked Nicole again.

"David!" Staci screamed.

"Look, Staci, shut the fuck up, okay? Yeah, I fucked up. Yes, I did wrong, but I can at least hold my daughter. Just one goddamn time. Damn! Can I do that?" David looked back at Nicole. "Can I?"

Nicole allowed him to pick up his daughter.

"Hello, beautiful. I'm your daddy."

I watched the tears roll down Nicole's face.

Staci stormed away as David placed baby Oliva on his chest.

"What's her name?"

"Oliva Nicole," I answered because Nicole couldn't.

"Hi, Olivia Nicole. I'm your daddy," David said to her.

He held her for a little while longer and inhaled the scent of her skin.

"Nicole, I'm sorry," he said finally, and then he kissed the baby's forehead. "I'm sorry, sweet girl. I'm so sorry."

He handed the baby to Nicole, and without saying anything else, David turned to walk away.

Finally, Nicole exhaled. And then she started to sob.

"It's okay, girl. It's okay. We got you. It's okay."

It took us all a minute to get our heads back in shopping mode, but finally, we did. And by the time we were done, we'd spent so much money that all of us had worked up an appetite.

We stopped and got pizza and wings on the way in.

"What do you have to drink in here?" I asked Nicole. "Nevermind. Damn, why do you have all of this vodka?"

"I was planning to get fucked up as soon as I dropped this baby," Nicole shrugged. "I've needed a drink so bad these past few months. Now, with these meds, I have to wait a little longer."

"Well, I'll have a drink or two for you."

I grabbed a cup and a bottle and plopped down on the couch.

"Call Tierra."

"Hola," she answered Dejah's phone.

"Bitch..." we all laughed. "What are you doing?"

"I'm out with Luis right now. What y'all doing?"

"Eating," Dejah said.

"And drinking!" I chimed in.

"Well, I'm going to have to miss the fun. I'm hoping to have dick breath and just a few minutes. I'll call y'all later."

"I swear, I hope God hurries up and give that girl somebody soon. I swear, she's gonna' jump into bed with the wrong one, one day, and..."

"Nope. Don't even speak that. She's going to be fine. Hell, we all are."

"I sure hope so."

"Aye, do y'all remember our first road trip together?"

Nicole smiled. "Girl, it was a complete disaster! I told myself I was never going anywhere with you bitches again."

"We had two flat tires, ran out of gas, and all, but we made it. And once we got to the casino, we had the time of our lives, didn't we?"

"We sure did! And we all won some money too," Dejah pointed out.

"Shit, not like Nicole did. You went home with some bank."

"And I've been pinching off of it for so long. I still have plenty of it left."

"Oh, I went through your stuff while you was out of it. Trust me, I know," Dejah laughed. "You told Tierra you had $25,000 saved. You have twice that."

"See, nosey, that's my savings-savings. Not my regular savings. With your nosey ass," Nicole laughed.

For the next two hours, we laughed, ate, and I got drunk.

Too drunk.

"Come on, drunk ass. I'll drive you home. We're leaving your car here," Dejah helped me up. "Nicole, are you sure you're going to be fine here with the baby alone?"

"Yes. I'll be fine."

"Byyyyeee Nicole," I sang going down the porch steps.

Dejah laughed and helped me into the car.

"I feel soooo gooooood," I dragged out my words as Dejah sped down the road.

"Good. Chile, I wish I could've gotten drunk with you."

"Dejah?"

"Yes."

I swallowed hard. "Do you think Tyrone is going to kill me?"

"What? Don't say shit like that, Bailey! Hell no. He better not touch you, or I'll kill him myself!"

Dejah turned up the radio, but I still pondered the thoughts in my head.

I can feel it.

Nothing is going to stop Tyrone…unless I'm dead.

***

Chapter 8

"Wake up, sleepyhead," Desmond chimed.

I groaned. "Owww."

"I hear you got drunk last night," Desmond chuckled.

"Uggh! I'm not getting out of bed today."

"Fine. Don't. I'll get Dejah to take me to get your car, and I'll drive it home from work."

"Okay."

"Love you. I'll see you later."

That's the last thing I heard before I passed out again.

The next time I opened my eyes, it was twelve in the afternoon.

"Hey, drunk ass," Dejah sat down next to me on the couch. "You were feeling good last night. Talking crazy and all."

"Lord, what did I say?"

"For starters, you think Tyrone wants to kill you."

"Oh, hell, I think that when I'm sober."

"Really?"

"Yep. Otherwise, what's the point in everything that he's doing?"

"I don't know. Some people just don't know how to let go."

"Yeah. Until the other person is dead."

Dejah rolled her eyes.

"Did everyone get dropped off on time?"

"Barely. The kids got to school on time, but I'm sure Desmond was late for work. He said he was going to be late for a meeting. You should've seen how fast he pulled out of Nicole's driveway."

"I've told him about his driving. He's probably called me by now. I left my phone in the room. Did you go in and check on Nicole and Olivia?"

"Yep. They were doing just fine. She said they had been up most of the night, so I didn't stay long so that she could go to sleep."

"I'm so happy for her. God knows I am."

"Me too. And she hasn't even mentioned the whole thing with David. Did you notice that?"

"Yep. I truly think she just doesn't care. I wouldn't want to have to deal with David's wife and the drama anyway. I would raise my baby all on my own. She will meet a good man who won't mind stepping up and helping her with Olivia."

"Yes. And this time she better ask him for his full name, birthday, and last four digits of his social so we can run a background check on his ass before she sleeps with him. Because I can't deal with this shit again."

"Really, you act like you're the one having to deal with it."

"Hell, it feels like it," Dejah laughed.

"Have you talk to Tyree?"

"Chile, don't get me started. He's still acting crazy. He's still acting like he don't want to get a divorce. I've been really thinking about it, you know, and it's just the right thing to do. For both of us. I've wasted enough of his time. He needs someone who can give him all the things he was looking for in me."

"Don't say that."

"But it's true," Dejah shrugged. "Now, hand me the remote."

Dejah turned on the tv to the news.

"Are you working from home today?"

I groaned. "I don't want to do anything today. I just want to lay here and…"

My eyes grew as big as golf balls.

"Turn up the TV, Dejah."

I stared at them pulling the car…my car…up from the side of the cliff.

"Oh, my God!" Dejah yelled.

"Dejah, tell me that's not my car. Tell me that's not my car!" I jumped to my feet. "Where's my phone? Where's my phone!"

I ran to my bedroom.

No calls from Desmond.

I called his phone over and over.

No answer.

I called his job.

They said he never showed up for work.

"Bailey, did you reach him? Did you reach him?"

I heard her, but I couldn't answer her.

My heart was breaking because I already knew the horrible, tragic truth.

Desmond.

My husband.

My friend.

My everything…is dead.

***

Two Weeks Later…

"Bailey, who was that on the phone?"

A single tear dropped from my eye.

"They got him."

"Who?"

"Tyrone. They got the man he hired to cut the brake line on my car at Nicole's that night to turn on him. He said Tyrone paid him to do it."

Desmond was speeding around curves as always, trying to get to work that day, and when he tapped the brakes, he found that the brakes on my car weren't working. He couldn't slow down. He couldn't stop. He couldn't do anything before flipping off a cliff.

Apparently, Tyrone had followed me to Nicole's house the day that we all went shopping. And seeing that I left my car behind, he had someone to cut the brake line. The intention was for me to get in an accident, but Desmond had gone to pick up my car instead.

He killed Desmond.

And I wish to God that he had killed me instead.

While the police were on the scene, there was plenty of fluid where my car had been parked at Nicole's that night. Had Desmond not been rushing to work, maybe he would've seen it and known that something was wrong. He would've at least checked to see where it was leaking from. And even if he decided to drive the car, maybe he would drove more careful. Maybe he wouldn't have been speeding. Maybe he wouldn't be dead.

For a long time, there seemed to be no evidence, but days after Desmond's death, a girl knocked on Nicole's door. She noticed the police tape and said she saw someone out there late one night, while she was sitting in her car smoking a cigarette. She'd just had a newborn and told her husband she wouldn't smoke anymore, but around 3 a.m., she snuck outside to her car to have a cigarette.

She said she noticed a man getting in a dark color van. She said she remembered because she always found it funny when men drove minivans. He wasn't around the car at the time, but she said the van was parked right behind the red Lexus. Her small tip helped cops trace back traffic footage, and they found the mechanic that Tyrone hired to tamper with my car.

For a while, he wouldn't admit to anything.

He wouldn't admit that he tampered with my car, and he wouldn't admit that Tyrone had anything to do with it. He simply said he was just in the neighborhood. He claimed he was innocent, and he told the police to prove that he did something wrong.

But today, finally, he came clean.

Now, finally, I can breathe, and my husband can rest in peace.

"He was going to kill me. I told you that Tyrone was going to kill me. I knew it. I knew he was going to try to. But he ended up killing Desmond instead." I shook my head. "And it's all my fault. All because I had an affair. I slept with the wrong man."

"Hey, now, you can't dwell on that. No one knew that this would happen. You can't spend the rest of your life blaming yourself. This is on Tyrone. Desmond's death is on Tyrone. And now, he's going to spend the rest of his life in jail." Dejah reassured me. "And Desmond would've rather it been him, than you. You know that."

"I just want him back, Dejah. I just want him back."

"I know you do, sweetie. I know."

Dejah hugged me.

No matter what she said, I still felt like it was all my fault. It was me who brought Tyrone into our lives in the first place. And now, I have to live with that and what he did to Desmond in the back of my mind forever.

If I had known all of this was going to happen, I would've just kept screwing him to keep the peace. I was trying to do the right thing. I was trying to save my marriage. That's all I wanted to do.

"Friend?" Dejah said.

"Yes."

"Can I ask you a favor?"

"Yes, Dej."

"I don't know if it's my pregnant nose or whatever, but could you please go wash your ass? Please. I'm begging you. I don't think you've washed since the funeral and…" Dejah gagged. "I think I'm about to throw up."

"Fuck you, Dejah!" I couldn't help but laugh.

She chuckled too. "Seriously, go on. Go get in the shower. The truth is out. Now…now it's time to heal."

I headed towards the bathroom feeling heavier than ever before, but once I got into the shower, I knew that Dejah was right.

Now, I know the truth.

I know what happened.

I know who did it.

Now I learn to breathe.

I learn to fly without Desmond by myself.

"I love you, Desmond," I whispered. "Forever. For always."

And I meant those words from the bottom of my heart.

***

"I think I'm cursed," Tierra frowned.

"What? Let me guess, Luis found someone else to marry?"

"How did you know?" Tierra huffed. "Like, I was giving him all this good African American pussy, and then he runs off and finds some white woman to marry him. I'm cursed. I'm just going to face the truth. I can't keep a man if my life depended on it."

We all howled in laughter. Tierra didn't understand what was so funny.

"It's not funny. Like, why can't I just find a good man, keep a good man, maybe have another baby or two, and just be happy?"

"See, that's the problem. Having a man isn't the only way to be happy."

"Girl, fuck you. It is to me."

We all laughed again.

"I see that belly forming," Nicole smiled at Dejah.

"Yes. It is ain't it?"

"Still mad that it's a boy?"

"Nah, it's okay. I got this little cutie to spoil," Dejah grabbed baby Oliva's finger.

Nicole hadn't had a choice but to bring her to our lunch.

"She's growing so much every day."

"You think you'll have another one?"

"Hell no!" Nicole yelled. "She's lucky she made it. But she's it. It'll be just me and her, forever if it has to be. I'll be just fine with that." Nicole smiled. "Bailey...you okay?"

I was tired of being asked that question.

Tyrone is in jail. He could get up to thirty years in prison for what he did. At first, they said he wasn't talking much. He was trying to say that the mechanic was lying and that he didn't know him, but the mechanic came with receipts. His wife was looking out the window when Tyrone gave him a bag of money. She'd asked him what it was for, and he said it was to work on a car for him. The money was still in the bag when the mechanic confessed, and it came out that Tyrone had gotten a chick to get a loan in her name just to pay the mechanic.

You have to be completely miserable to get a loan, to pay someone, to tamper with someone's car, just to hurt them because they won't sleep with you anymore.

Nevertheless, the police had more than enough to make a case against Tyrone even if he never confesses to what he did.

All I know is I'll be okay for sure when the jury finds him guilty. I heard he was offered a plea deal for twenty years. If only he would confess. Either way, twenty or thirty years in prison wouldn't bring my husband back, but at least Tyrone would be losing his life too.

In a sense.

"I'm okay," I lied.

I'm not sure if I'll ever really be okay again.

I'm not sure if I'll ever be truly happy again.

I'm not sure if I'll ever find love again.

I feel like I'm in a bad dream.

It's like...what now?

What am I supposed to do without Desmond?

What am I supposed to say to my kids when they miss him?

I can never get the image of him lying in that casket out of my head. I know that he would've wanted it to be him, instead of me, but he just wasn't supposed to die.

We were supposed to be happy together.

Forever.

And now, I have to figure out how to get through the rest of my life without him.

Since he's been gone, when I'm not crying, I'm writing. I'm writing full of grief and pain. I'm writing full of anger. Desmond was my business fan, so in a way, I feel like I'm writing for him too.

I just hope he's able to look down from Heaven and be proud of me. I hope in his last moments that he didn't hate me for ruining our lives. I hope he felt love for me.

"This has been a hell of a year," Dejah pointed out. "For all of us, in our own way. But we've made it through. We're still here. We're still sisters. I'm rocking with you ladies through the thick and the thin. Through the unhappily ever after."

Dejah raised her glass.

The rest of us did the same.

"To unhappily ever after," she smiled. "Shit, at least that's what it's looking like for all of us right now."

"To unhappily ever after."

We clanked our glasses together, took a sip of our drinks, and then we all burst into laughter.

She's right.

Life has been a bitch, to all of us, the past few months, but at least I got them to get through it all with. And watching them talk and laugh, I realized that Dejah had just given me the title to my next best-selling book.

Unhappily Ever After.

Yes, that sounds about right.

****

The END

CPSIA information can be obtained
at www.ICGtesting.com
Printed in the USA
LVHW011952230621
690958LV00016B/1619